KALONA'S
FALL

KALONA'S FALL

P. C. CAST and KRISTIN CAST

ST. MARTIN'S GRIFFIN

NEW YORK

This is a work of fiction. All of the characters, organizations, and events portrayed in this novel are either products of the authors' imaginations or are used fictitiously.

www.stmartins.com

Interior illustrations by Aura Dalian

Library of Congress Cataloging-in-Publication Data

Cast, P. C.
    Kalona's fall : a House of Night novella / P. C. Cast and Kristin Cast. — First U.S. edition.
        pages cm

    ISBN 978-1-250-04611-6 (hardcover)
    ISBN 978-1-4668-4627-2 (e-book)
    1. Redbird, Zoey (Fictitious character)—Fiction.   2. Magic—Fiction.   I. Cast, Kristin.   II. Title.

    PS3603.A869K35 2014
    813'.6—dc23

                                        2014015465

St. Martin's Griffin books may be purchased for educational, business, or promotional use. For information on bulk purchases, please contact Macmillan Corporate and Premium Sales Department at 1-800-221-7945, extension 5442, or write specialmarkets@macmillan.com.

First Edition: August 2014

10   9   8   7   6   5   4   3   2   1

For all of you who asked,
"What really happened to Kalona?"

ACKNOWLEDGMENTS

Thank you to my publishing family. I appreciate you very much! A big hug to my illustrator, Aura Dalian. YOU ARE AWESOME! Christine—you are the best brainstormer, EVER. As always, thank you to my agent and friend Meredith Bernstein.

1.

INTRIGUE BEGAT CURIOSITY,
AND CURIOSITY BEGAT EXPLORATION...

Once upon a time, long, long ago, there was only the Divine Energy of the universe. Energy was neither good nor bad, light nor dark, male nor female—it simply existed, a maelstrom of possibilities, clashing, joining, and growing. As Energy grew, it evolved. As it evolved, it created.

First came the creation of the realms of the Otherworld— endless vistas filled with the dreams of Divinity. These realms were so beautiful that they inspired Energy to continue creating, and from the womb of each of the Otherworld realms great solar systems were born, tangible reflections of the Otherworld Old Magick.

The Divine Energy of the universe was so pleased by its creations that it began to shift and change as vortexes of power within itself, mothlike, were drawn to the different universes. Some Energy was content and rested, eternally existing in a swirling orbit of stars and moons and beautiful, but empty, planets.

Some Energy destroyed its creations, more content with itself than with possibilities.

And some Energy continued to change, evolve, and create.

In one Otherworld realm the Divine Energy was particularly questing and precocious, restless and joyful, because more than anything it desired companionship. So, from within the verdant groves and sapphire lakes of the Otherworld, the Divine fashioned fabulous beings and breathed life into them. The breath of the Divine carried with it immortality and consciousness. The Divine named these beings Gods, Goddesses, and Fey. He granted the Gods and Goddesses dominion over all the Otherworld realms, and tasked the Fey with being their servants.

Many of the immortal beings scattered throughout the endless Otherworld realms, but those who remained pleased the Divine greatly. To them the Divine gifted an additional dominion over all other immortals, that of the stewardship of one particular planet in their system—a planet that intrigued the Divine Energy because it reflected the green-and-blue beauty of the Otherworld.

Intrigue begat curiosity, and curiosity begat exploration, until finally the Divine could not resist stroking the surface of the green-and-sapphire planet. The planet awoke, naming itself Earth. Earth beckoned to the Divine, inviting it within her lush lands and her sweet, soothing waters.

Filled with wonder, the Gods and Goddesses watched.

Enchanted by his own creation, Divine Energy joined with Earth. She pleased him greatly, but Energy cannot be long contained. Earth understood and accepted his nature, never loving him less for that which could not be changed. Before he left her to rove the universe, seeking more companionship, Divine Energy gave the Earth his most precious gift—the magick that was the power of creation.

Young Earth, fertile and sultry, began to create.

Earth sowed the lands and the oceans with her gift of creation, and from them evolved such a magnitude of creatures that the Gods and Goddesses from the watching Otherworld began to visit her often, reveling in the diversity of the living Earth.

Earth welcomed the immortals, children of her beloved Divine. She loved them so fondly that she was inspired to design a very special creation. From her bosom, she formed and then breathed life into beings that she fashioned in the very image of the Gods and Goddesses, naming them humans. Though Mother Earth was not able to gift her children with immortality—that was a gift only Divine Energy could bestow—she placed within each of them a spark of the Divinity that had been shared with her, ensuring that even though their bodies must always return to the earth from which they had been made, their consciousness would continue eternally in the form of spirit, so that they could be reborn again and again to Mother Earth.

Created in their image, Earth's children enchanted the Gods and Goddesses. The Gods and Goddesses vowed to watch over them and to share the Otherworld with the Divine spirits within them when the inevitable happened, and their mortal bodies died.

At first all was well; humans prospered and multiplied. They were grateful to Mother Earth, each culture holding her sacred. The Gods and Goddesses visited Earth's children often, and humans revered them as Divine.

Mother Earth watched, noticing which of the Divine's children were benevolent, and which were impetuous. Which of them were forgiving, and which were vengeful. Which of them were kind and which were cruel.

When the immortals were benevolent and forgiving and kind, Mother Earth was pleased, and showed her pleasure in fertile lands, quenching rains, and crops aplenty.

When the immortals were impetuous and vengeful and cruel, Mother Earth turned her face from them and there was drought and famine and plague.

The impetuous, vengeful, cruel deities became bored with drought and famine and plague and stopped visiting the living Earth.

Mother Earth was satisfied, and she retreated within herself, resting from the strain of creation, sleeping for eons uncountable. When next she awoke, she looked for the children of the Divine, and was hardly aware of their presence at all.

Calling Air to her, Mother Earth sent a message to the

Otherworld, beseeching the children of her beloved to remember their vow, and inviting them to return to her.

Only one immortal answered her plea.

The Goddess manifested during a clear night when the moon was almost full, on a rugged isle yet to be named. As Mother Earth became conscious of the Goddess, she saw the immortal sitting before a grove, her delicate hand outstretched toward a curious wildcat.

"Where are the other children of the Divine?" Mother Earth's voice was the sloughing of hawthorn leaves in the grove.

The Goddess lifted her shoulder in a gesture that Mother Earth found surprisingly childlike. "They have gone."

The ground trembled in response to Mother Earth's surprise. "All? How could they all have gone?"

"They said they were bored and became restless." The Goddess shook her head and her long, fair hair glistened in the moonlight, changing from blond to silver.

The leaves of the grove trees shivered. "So like their father," Mother Earth whispered sadly. "Why must they all leave me?"

The Goddess sighed. "I do not know. I do not understand how they could ever be bored here." She stroked the wildcat that had curled lovingly around her feet. "There is something new every day. Imagine, just yesterday I did not know this wonderful creature existed."

Pleased, Mother Earth warmed the breeze that carried

her voice from the grove. "You must have been formed from one of his more tangible dreams."

"Yes," the Goddess said wistfully. "I just wish more of his dreams had been like me. It is . . ." She hesitated, as if unable to decide whether to continue.

"It is what?" Mother Earth prompted.

"Lonely," she admitted softly. "Especially when there are no other beings like me."

Mother Earth felt the Goddess's sadness and, taking pity on her, she called awake the grove, where from the moss and dirt, leaves and flowers, Mother Earth took tangible form.

The Goddess smiled at her. As beautiful as the gossamer wings of a butterfly, Mother Earth smiled back, asking, "What is your name, Goddess?"

"Humans are calling me many names." The Goddess gave the wildcat a final caress and then straightened, spreading wide her arms. "Some call me Sarasvati." Her body shifted in form, changing skin from light to dark, hair from fair as moonlight to the black of a raven's wing as another pair of slender arms suddenly appeared. Still smiling, the Goddess continued, "Nidaba is the name some of your children whisper in their prayers." Again, the Goddess shifted form, growing wings and replacing her feet with talons. "And not far from this very island, they have begun to know me as Breo-saighead, bringer of fire and justice." With that pronouncement, the Goddess took the form of a beautiful woman with hair the color of flame, her white skin decorated by brilliant sapphire tribal tattoos.

Delighted, Mother Earth clapped her hands, and sleeping butterflies awoke to cavort around her. "But I know you! I have watched these Goddesses for countless ages. You are kind and benevolent and just."

"I am. I am also alone." The fire faded from her hair, and once again the Goddess looked like a fair-haired maiden, innocent and sweetly sad.

"Which name would you have me call you?" Mother Earth asked, wanting to distract her from her melancholy.

The Goddess considered, and then answered, rather shyly, "There is one name I like more than the others— Nyx. It reminds me of night, and I do so love the peacefulness of night and the beauty of moonlight."

As she spoke, Mother Earth saw that her form changed only slightly. She still looked young, but she had lifted her chin, smiling up at the moon, delicate, filigreed tattooing glowed silver and sapphire over her skin making her look mysterious and incredibly beautiful. With hardly a thought, Mother Earth called magick from the night sky and scattered it on the Goddess, so that it settled upon her as a headdress of glistening moonlight and stars.

"Oh! That is lovely! May I keep it?" the Goddess said, twirling around girlishly.

"*You* are lovely Nyx. And you may keep it on one condition—that instead of following the others, you do not desert my children and me."

Nyx went very still. Her girlishness fell away from her until Mother Earth was looking into the eyes of a mature Goddess who wore wisdom and power as surely as she did the mantle of moonlight. When Nyx spoke, Mother Earth heard within her voice the power of Divinity. "You need not tether me here with bribery. Such tricks are not worthy of you. When you created humans I vowed that I would watch over them and make a place for that within them that remains eternal and Divine. I never break a vow."

Slowly, Mother Earth bowed her head to Nyx. "Forgive me."

"With all my heart," Nyx said.

Mother Earth stood, and with the rustle of wind sweeping through a meadow of tall grass, she moved to Nyx and cupped the Goddess's face between her verdurous palms. "And now I freely give to you a gift—one that is worthy of us both. Henceforth from this night, I grant you command over my five elements: Air, Fire, Water, Earth, and Spirit. Call on any, and they shall answer, doing your bidding eternally." Mother Earth bent and kissed Nyx on her forehead.

From the center of Nyx's forehead a perfect crescent moon appeared, and on either side of her face, spreading down the Goddess's beautiful body, a filigree pattern appeared, bearing signs and symbols that represented all five elements.

Nyx lifted her slender arm, studying her new Marks in appreciation. "That is as special as are each of the elements. I will treasure your gift eternally." Nyx's girlish smile returned. "For that I also thank you with all my heart. After tonight I do not feel so alone, nor so frightened."

"Frightened? But whatever could frighten an immortal created by the Divine?"

Nyx brushed a strand of silver hair from her face, and Mother Earth noticed her hand trembled.

"Darkness." The Goddess whispered the word.

Mother Earth smiled as she sat beneath the hawthorn tree nearest Nyx. "But you just spoke about the peace and beauty of night. How, then, could darkness frighten you?"

"The night could never frighten me; it is not literal darkness of which I speak, but an intangible in which I sense a seeking, growing power that knows nothing of peace and joy and beauty—that knows nothing of love." Nyx spoke softly but earnestly. "It has not fully entered the Otherworld yet, but I have sensed it often here, on the mortal realm. I think it grows stronger the longer I am alone."

Mother Earth considered her words carefully before she responded. "I sense the truth in your fear. That this Darkness has worsened with your loneliness tells me that what has happened to you is affecting my realm—and quite possibly it will spread to your Otherworld. Goddess, I am afraid our realms have become unbalanced."

"How shall we restore what has been lost?"

Mother Earth smiled. "I believe our first step has already been taken. Let us agree to be friends. As long as I exist you shall never truly be alone again."

Nyx flung her arms around Mother Earth. "Thank you!"

Mother Earth returned her embrace. "Dearest child, you have brought me much joy this night. Will you meet me again? Here, in this grove, three nights hence when the moon is full?"

"It would be my pleasure." Nyx stood and inclined her head regally to Mother Earth before, grinning, she bent and scooped the wildcat into her arms. In an explosion of glittering silver stars, she and the beast disappeared.

While she watched the trail of stars fade, Mother Earth rested against the skin of a hawthorn tree, thinking . . . thinking . . . thinking . . .

For three days and three nights Mother Earth did not move.

On the third day the grove was so infused with the magick of her presence it drew such bountiful sunlight that the brush covering the little island began to bloom purple with joy.

Mother Earth smiled upon the sun, and the sun quickened in response.

As night fell on the third day, the moon, drawn to the grove by the magick of her presence, beamed so fully on the little island that the rugged clumps of rock that dotted the landscape changed color permanently, reflecting the white of moonlight, infused with the magick of night.

Mother Earth smiled upon the moon, and the moon quickened in response.

With a small sound of satisfaction, Mother Earth knew what she must do for this last, this only, this most special Goddess, Nyx.

2.

IT IS BECAUSE YOU DO NOT ASK THAT I WISH
TO REWARD YOU, GREAT GODDESS…

Nyx dressed carefully for her visit with Mother Earth, directing the little Fey skeeaed, the most godlike of the creatures created from the wisps of Divine Energy that circled restlessly in the atmosphere of the Otherworld, to take special care with the draping of her silver gown.

"Thank you for choosing such a perfect color, L'ota!" she told the skeeaed as its sinuous body circled the Goddess, whispering *"Beautiful moon color"* in its liquid voice.

When a dryad began to weave ivy through her long, dark hair, Nyx exclaimed in pleasure, "Oh! That is a lovely touch! Mother Earth will so appreciate it."

Only the skeeaeds had the ability to speak, but the little dryad turned deep lavender and trilled in pleasure at the Goddess's praise.

Then the Goddess turned her head this way and that, examining her reflection in her onyx-framed mirror.

"But the ivy is hidden in the darkness of my hair. I want Mother Earth to see it—to know that I have adorned myself in respect for her!" With a wave of her hand, Nyx changed her visage, taking on blond hair so silver that the green of the ivy seemed luminous.

"Perfect!" Nyx smiled in delight.

Another Fey, a coblyn who mined jewels from the Otherworld caves, appeared. Bowing respectfully, he held forth a necklace fashioned from a waterfall of glittering quartz crystals.

"Your gift touches my heart," Nyx said, holding up the thick length of her hair so that the Fey could place the necklace on her. "I hope it touches Mother Earth's heart as well." Nyx caressed the crystals, thinking how desperately she wished for companionship. She adored the Fey, but they were more spirit and element than flesh. Nyx did long for true companionship . . . the touch of another immortal.

Nyx felt the sadness that radiated from the Fey in response to her lonely thoughts and was instantly sorry she'd given in to melancholy. She was the last of the immortals and she knew the Fey doted on her from more than just the affection shared between them. Like Mother Earth, they feared she would follow the others—would forsake her vow and leave this realm.

"Never." Nyx's voice was soft, but she spoke with finality, caressing a concerned skeeaed much as she stroked the wildcat, who now followed her everywhere. "You have nothing to fear," she reassured L'ota and the gathering Fey. "I will never break that vow or any vow I ever make—not throughout all of eternity. Now, please help settle in place the headdress of moonlight and stars that was my gift from Mother Earth, and worry no more!"

The Fey danced around her, coloring the air with happiness as they rejoiced in their Goddess's fidelity.

In the corner of the Goddess's chamber, within the deepest of the shadows, something dark quivered. As if it cringed away from the contagious happiness of the Fey, it slid, unseen, from the room.

Mother Earth was waiting for Nyx. She had already taken form and was standing before the grove, breathing deeply of the fragrant evening primrose from which she had fashioned her hair. She stroked the smooth, curvaceous skin she had fashioned for her body from the purest of clays. She called Air to her, directing it to lift the diaphanous gown adoring silkworms had created for her. She knew she looked especially alluring. The sun had beamed down on her grove from dawn to dusk, and now, enrapt, the moon watched.

Mother Earth was pleased.

The Goddess manifested when the moon, full and attentive, was high in the clear night's sky.

"Nyx! You delight me! You've chosen my ivy for your hair. It complements the headdress as flowers complement a meadow."

The Goddess had chosen to wear the visage of a young girl with silver-blond hair and fair skin, and the familiar delicate tattoos decorating her smooth shoulders. Mother Earth smiled as Nyx flushed in pleasure.

"Thank you! The Fey helped adorn me. They are clever and considerate, though they rarely speak." Nyx touched the crystal necklace. "A coblyn made this for me."

"Why, that is as lovely as your headdress! They must be very special creatures. I am intrigued to learn about them, as I have created nothing like them. Nyx, would you give them leave to visit me? I would welcome the presence of the Fey."

"Of course! I'm sure they would be delighted. Would you mind if they allowed themselves to be seen by your children? I think it would make them less lonely, though I must warn you, some of the Fey can be rather mischievous."

"Oh, do not let that concern you. My human children could use a little divine mischief. Sometimes I think mankind has become far too serious. They forget the special magick that can be found in fun-loving mischief and laughter." Mother Earth's own laughter caused the sleeping bluebells in the meadow before the grove to wake and burst into full bloom.

"Those flowers are so beautiful! The Fey especially love bright colors. Thank you, Mother Earth." Nyx and Mother Earth smiled at each other and the isle glowed with reflected joy.

All the while the moon watched.

"Nyx, would you tell me more about the Fey? I have never met one."

"Oh, yes! There are so many types of them."

Mother Earth's smile turned satisfied as she stroked a white boulder that had been saturated by moonlight and called moss to carpet it. "Come, sit beside me." While Nyx gracefully settled herself, Mother Earth gently waved her hand through the grass that grew in tufts around the boulder. Instantly, several plants sprung to life, producing white, trumpet-shaped flowers. Thanking each plant, Mother Earth gently plucked the blossoms free and offered one to Nyx. "Sip slowly—the nectar is as delicious as it is potent."

Sipping from the living chalice, Nyx began describing the different types of Fey to Mother Earth, who listened, attentive and smiling, until the moon reluctantly began to depart. Where the horizon met the gray-blue waters surrounding the island, the approaching sun caused the sky to blush.

"I had no idea it was so late. You must forgive me. It has been too long since I have had an opportunity to practice conversation."

"Lovely Goddess, I have enjoyed myself more tonight than I have in eons. And I have a confession to make: you are not to blame for the length of our conversation. I kept you with me purposefully until now. I wish to reward your fidelity."

Nyx looked startled. "But that is not necessary. Mother Earth, I will remain and watch over your children. I have given you my vow. I will not ask for a reward for keeping my word."

"It is because you do not ask that I wish to reward you." Looking inordinately pleased with herself, Mother Earth stood. Turning to the east, toward the rising sun, she lifted her face to the fading moon.

"But what—" Nyx began.

Mother Earth smiled fondly over her shoulder at the Goddess. "This gift is not to tether you to me. I trust your fidelity. What I create tonight is fashioned from friendship and appreciation. Tonight my only purpose is to end your loneliness by bringing you joy." Then, with the young Goddess looking on in curiosity, Mother Earth raised her arms.

"Moon, harken to me before you depart my sky. Mother Earth doth call to thee!" She dropped her chin so that her gaze focused from the sky above to the coral tip of the dawning sun and said, "Sun, harken to me before you climb too high. Mother Earth doth call to thee!"

For a moment nothing happened, but Mother Earth did not despair. She tossed back her fragrant hair and called Air to her again. The element caressed her, revealing her lush beauty. She called Fire to her so that she glowed with living flame. She called Water, and suddenly the sea that surrounded the island stilled and became a liquid mirror, reflecting Mother Earth's loveliness. She called Spirit and wisps of power washed over her, enhancing her already preternaturally luminous form.

Confidently, Mother Earth waited.

The moon responded first, forever changing Nyx's destiny.

As if a pebble had disturbed the surface of a sleeping pond, the fading moon shivered and then brightened from gray to silver. Far above the grove, a deep voice echoed from the sky.

The moon doth harken to Mother Earth's call. What is thy will? Mighty moon is eager to fulfill.

Just then the sun lifted above the watery horizon, shining the yellow and pink of dawn on the grassy ground before the grove. From over the stilled waves, a voice, equally as deep and powerful, echoed.

The sun doth harken to Mother Earth's call. What is it thee requires? The power of sun shall fulfill your desires.

Mother Earth's smile was as promising and fertile as a meadow in spring.

"Mighty moon and powerful sun, twin guardians of my sky, I ask a favor from each of you."

And what do I gain in return? Both voices spoke at the same time.

Mother Earth's smile did not dim. She lifted her face to the moon. "To you, mighty moon, I give dominion over my oceans. After this day, the tides will follow your will."

I accept your gift. The moon's voice rumbled, deepening with pleasure.

Mother Earth gazed fully on the rising sun. "To you, powerful sun, I give dominion over my northernmost lands. For all of summer, you shall reign there supreme, and never set."

I accept your gift, the sun agreed eagerly.

"You have each spoken vow to me—thus you are

bound—so mote it be!" proclaimed Mother Earth. "Know first that what I ask is not for myself, but for Nyx, the ever-faithful Goddess who kept her vow and remained, the last of the children of the Divine."

There was a ripple in the air as the moon transmitted surprise. *They are all gone? All of the Gods and Goddesses?*

"All but this one," Mother Earth said.

The air around the grove heated with the sun's shock. *But it seems only yesterday that the Gods and Goddesses frolicked below and above.*

"To me as well," Mother Earth agreed. Then she turned, beckoning for the pale, silent Goddess to stand beside her. Taking Nyx's hand, she continued. "But for Nyx, known by many names to my children, those days and nights have been long and empty."

Were I not already bound by vow to aid, I would willingly reward this lone and lovely Goddess, said the moon.

Nyx's smile was filled with shy delight. "Thank you, mighty moon. I have long relished your ever-changing face and your pure silver light."

I, too, am pleased to aid one so fair and faithful, said the sun.

"And thank you, powerful sun. Your summer warmth has brought me countless days of pleasure," Nyx said, bowing to the east.

"Wonderful! Then let us make this dream so!" cried Mother Earth.

"How? I am sorry, but I do not understand," said Nyx.

"Tell me, sweet Goddess, if you could have a companion,

brought to life by the might of the moon and the power of the sun, what would you have this companion be?"

With no hesitation, Nyx answered, "He would be warrior and lover, playmate and friend."

"Very well then, that is what you shall have." Mother Earth squeezed Nyx's hand before releasing it and returning her attention to the listening moon and sun.

She raised her arms again, and this time began to turn her hands gently, gracefully, as if sifting through invisible threads around her.

"Once more, I use that which the Divine granted me. Power of Creation, I call thee forth from the sky! Couple with the might of the moon and the power of the sun, and bring forth immortal life as companion to my faithful Goddess!"

Mother Earth's voice took on a rhythmic cadence as she spoke the spell:

> *I am She*
> *Loved so well by*
> *The Divine*
> *Creation is my gift*
>
> *I am She*
> *Cherished so well by*
> *The Divine*
> *My call from Earth to Sky shall lift*
>
> *I am she*
> *Beloved so well by*

The Divine
Moon! Sun! Sky! Join true—join sure—join swift!

Create warrior and lover, playmate and friend.
Do not leave my Goddess companionless, lonely with
*   no end!*

The sky above the grove came alive with currents of glistening magick ancient as the Divine—unending Energy bound to obey the Earth's command. It multiplied and divided, pulsing with the light of creation so brightly that even Mother Earth and the Goddess Nyx had to shield their eyes. Then the currents swept up, up, up to the fading moon, and up, up, up to the rising sun. The moon and the sun blazed, pulsing with the joining so beautifully that Mother Earth thought it seemed that the sky kissed first the moon, and then the sun.

There was an explosion of light above and around Mother Earth and Nyx, and then all was still.

The sun continued to rise, silently, distantly. The moon faded into the heavens.

Mother Earth had just begun to frown and was considering how she would penalize both moon and sun for not fulfilling their vows when she heard Nyx's surprised gasp.

Mother Earth shifted her gaze. She had been staring up, expecting a being to float down from the sky. But her expectations had been incorrect. The beings were already there, kneeling before Nyx.

In shock, Mother Earth watched as two godlings fashioned from the joining of the sky and the moon, and the sun and the moon, lifted their faces and gazed with utter adoration at their Goddess.

"They have wings!" Nyx exclaimed.

"And there are two of them," Mother Earth said, furrowing her brow in consternation. "Nyx, this did not go exactly as I had planned."

"I think they are perfect!" said the Goddess.

3.

SHE WOULD BE A MIGHTY ENEMY...

Newly created, Kalona opened his eyes. His first sight was that of Nyx. He didn't know her name then. All he knew was that her beauty arrowed into him and lodged somewhere so deeply that it made him unable to speak.

She approached him first, though he was hardly aware of the other being kneeling beside him. She held out her hand to him and said the first words he ever heard: "I am the Goddess Nyx, and I welcome you with all of my heart."

Her voice was sweet and musical and soothing. Kalona took her slender hand carefully within his own much larger one, noticing the unique beauty of their contrasting skins—his darker, burnished, rougher, while hers was soft and pale and utterly flawless.

Still, he couldn't seem to speak. Her smile had his blood heating and his body feeling flushed.

"And what is your name?" she asked him.

"Kalona," he blurted.

"Kalona. What a beautiful name! Your wings are the silver of a full moon. You must be the son of the moon," she said.

"I am," he said, without stopping to wonder at how he knew it. "And I was fashioned for you."

Her smiled blazed, and Kalona could feel his heartbeat increase.

"Goddess Nyx, I am Erebus, son of the golden sun. Hence the reason my wings are *not* the color of moonlight. I, too, have been fashioned for you." The other winged godling stood. "Excuse me, brother, but I cannot allow you to keep the Goddess to yourself," he quipped as he stepped around Kalona, gently pulling Nyx's hand from his before Erebus bowed with a flourish of golden wings.

Nyx turned her luminous smile to Erebus and her delighted laughter seemed to sparkle in the grove around them. "Erebus! I welcome the son of the sun with all of my heart as well."

"Lovely Goddess, have a care for how much of your heart you give away. You give Kalona all—you give me all. Surely one of us will come up short?" Erebus's golden eyes flashed as mischievously as his smile.

Kalona frowned at Erebus and found himself having to grit his teeth against a feral growl. He should not dare to speak to the Goddess thus! Kalona would have liked to knock that cocky smile from the godling's face!

"I do not think you should begin this relationship by admonishing your Goddess, young Erebus, especially as I can see it incites your brother's ire." Kalona hadn't even noticed the other being until she began to speak, moving forward so that she positioned herself between Nyx and himself and Erebus, almost as if she thought the Goddess needed protection against them. Kalona narrowed his eyes at this lesser woman, ready to correct her, to tell her that Nyx would never need protection against him! He would never—could never—hurt her! But the woman's eyes caught his before he could speak, and a warning in their dark depths silenced him.

"Kalona, Erebus, please greet my friend, Mother Earth. You must thank her, as it is she who enabled your creation!" Nyx said breathlessly.

Erebus's smile was charming, his voice deep and gentle, as he bowed to her saying, "Great Mother, I greet and thank you, and I ask that you forget my first, mistaken attempt at humor. I assure you that my intention was not to admonish my Goddess, though I admit to finding it amusing that I was able to so easily incite my brother's ire."

"Precocious, so precocious!" Mother Earth smiled at Erebus as she spoke, embracing him gently and making it obvious that she liked the sun godling's precociousness.

Kalona stood and bowed deeply, respectfully. "I greet you, Mother Earth, and thank you for the role you played in my conception."

"You are welcome, Kalona." She embraced him as well, but Kalona thought it was with much less warmth than she had embraced his brother. Mother Earth stepped back and addressed the three of them. "So you each acknowledge that I do have a maternal responsibility here," said Mother Earth.

"Indeed you do, my friend," Nyx responded readily. "And I shall eternally thank you for it."

"Eternity is such a long, long time," Mother Earth said, studying Kalona and Erebus in turn. "I suppose you will want to take them back to the Otherworld with you?"

Kalona's gaze locked with Nyx's. He saw that her cheeks had pinked alluringly, and though her gaze did not leave his, her voice softened, seeming almost shy. "Yes, I will."

"Today?"

"Today!" Nyx said, nodding her head, still not looking away from Kalona.

"The Otherworld," Kalona said, finding his voice. "Even the name sounds magickal."

Nyx rewarded him with an intimate smile. "It is beautiful, much like this planet, only it is filled with ancient, Divine magick and powers that are sometimes difficult for even me to wield. Such powers can be exhausting," she finished, suddenly sounding older and tired.

"My Goddess, I will help you wield the powers that exhaust you," Kalona said, taking an eager step toward her.

"And yet it is not your place to wield the Old Magick of Nyx's Otherworld," Mother Earth said, also taking a step closer.

Kalona felt the heat of Mother Earth's power, and of her displeasure. Their gazes met, hers even more unflinching than his. *She would be a mighty enemy* . . . The knowledge echoed through his mind.

Kalona backed down and bowed his head slightly in acknowledgment of Mother Earth's might.

Erebus seemed not to notice Mother Earth's intense displeasure. His voice was as light as his smile. "What would we want with Nyx's magick? There is magick aplenty in the Divine Ether that created us. Should we need power, we have but to call on it. It must answer us, as that is our blood right as sons of the Divine. Great Mother, our matriarch, I assure you, my brother and I have no desires other than to serve Nyx."

"Remember, Mother Earth, the winged immortals were created *for* me and not *against* me," Nyx said, agreeing with the golden-winged immortal.

"Yes, I know. They were created by me." Mother Earth was not so easily placated. She faced off against Kalona and Erebus. "You were created by me to serve Nyx; therefore, it is *my* responsibility to see you are willing and able to fulfill your twin destinies as warrior and lover, playmate and friend. Nyx, do you agree that this is my responsibility?"

"My gratitude is such that I will never debate responsibilities with you. Instead I freely acknowledge that you are Mother and Creator of all of this." Nyx paused, sweeping her arm gracefully in a gesture that took in the whole of the earth, as well as the two winged immortals. "Simply tell me how you propose to fulfill your maternal responsibility. I shall not naysay you."

Kalona felt his stomach tighten as Mother Earth continued to study them carefully, as if searching for flaws.

"I take you at your word, Nyx. This is what I propose," Mother Earth said, sending Nyx a maternal and very satisfied-looking smile. "Under my supervision, your two winged immortals must complete three tasks each for you, proving that they are powerful and wise and loyal enough to be worthy of you."

"That sounds delightful, doesn't it?" Nyx said.

"Absolutely," Erebus said.

"I look forward to proving my worth to you," Kalona said.

"Delightful!" Nyx repeated, meeting Kalona's gaze.

"Then we begin immediately," Mother Earth said, cooling the heat that Nyx's gaze had been building in Kalona's blood.

"Immediately?" Nyx said, obviously less pleased than Mother Earth.

"Oh, child." Mother Earth put her arm around the Goddess. "Savor these first, wondrous steps. The magick of discovery is always sweeter if it has been earned."

Nyx brightened. "You have been right thus far. I trust you!" The Goddess turned back to Kalona and Erebus. "I ask that you follow Mother Earth's edicts as if they were my own. She is my true, dear friend." Nyx looked from them to Mother Earth. "What is it you would have them do?"

"There are to be three tasks. For each of them I would have Kalona and Erebus choose an element—three of the magickal five: Air, Fire, Water, Earth, and Spirit. Along with the element of their choosing, I gift them with a wisp of creation energy. Mix my gift with the power of the Divine that Erebus has so recently claimed as their birthright." She paused and bowed her head slightly to Erebus in acknowledgment. "And they must each create something *here*"—her hand swept out, a gesture that mirrored Nyx's—"that will delight you *there*." Mother Earth lifted her arm, pointing up into the brilliant blue of the morning sky.

"What a wonderful idea!" Nyx said, clapping her hands together happily.

Kalona frowned. "Creation through elements? Fashioned here and enjoyed in the Otherworld? I do not intend impertinence, Mother Earth, but how are we to complete these tasks without knowing anything about the Earth or the Otherworld?"

Mother Earth waved her hands dismissively. "You carry the immortality of Divine Energy—that which created us all. Look within. You already know the Otherworld. The rest is simple *if* you take the time to learn about my earth and my elements."

"And we know our Goddess," Erebus said, smiling fondly at Nyx. "We were created knowing our Goddess. Pleasing her is our pleasure!"

Kalona growled again.

Mother Earth narrowed dark eyes on him, giving him a hard look, as if she were truly a mother and he her errant child.

"Which element will you choose first?" Nyx asked, seemingly oblivious to the tension between Kalona and Mother Earth.

Kalona was certain the Goddess had spoken to him, but it was his brother who answered, "Air, of course. It was from Air that we were fashioned for you. It is only right that Air continues to delight you."

"An excellent choice, Erebus," Mother Earth said. "Until

you each call into being your creation, I grant you dominion over Air! So I have spoken; so mote it be!" A whoosh of wind washed over them, punctuating her words. Then she took Nyx's hand and wrapped it through her arm. "Come, Nyx, let us leave your immortals to the first of their tests while we drink more nectar and you introduce me to some of your interesting little Fey."

"But, what exactly are we are supposed to create?" Kalona asked, hating the desperation he heard in his voice.

Mother Earth glanced over her shoulder at him. "If you are clever enough to claim a place beside this lovely, faithful Goddess, you are clever enough to figure that out on your own—unless you fail the test, Kalona."

"I will not fail," Kalona said through gritted teeth.

"But if you do fail," Mother Earth said, "you will not be allowed access to the Otherworld—not until you pass all three tests. Agreed?"

"Willingly agreed," Erebus said.

"Agreed," Kalona said, though reluctantly.

"But I am quite sure you will not fail," Nyx said. Her words were balm to him until she turned her gaze from him to his brother. "Neither of you will fail me. And I cannot wait to see your creations!"

"Oh, one last thing," Mother Earth said. "My world is populated by humans, mortals fashioned by me in the image of the immortals. They are beloved by me. Have a care with them. No doubt they will mistake you for Gods. If you must interact with them, be quite certain that they know it is a *mistake*. You are warrior and lover, friend and playmate—you are not Gods. Do you understand me?"

The winged immortals murmured tandem assurances that they did, indeed, understand Mother Earth.

"Good! When you have gained enough knowledge and are ready, use Air to summon me. Nyx will accompany me. As your Goddess she has the right to judge your creations. I wish both of you luck in your endeavors," Mother Earth said.

"And I look forward to welcoming both of you to the Otherworld when your tests have been completed," Nyx said, smiling at Kalona and Erebus in turn.

Then, changing quickly from divine to girlish, the two women put their heads together, one as luminous as the full moon, the other as dark and mysterious as the ground on which they stood. Giggling and whispering, they disappeared into the verdant grove.

Kalona stared after his Goddess, wishing nothing so much as to rush to Nyx and pull her from Mother Earth—pull her away from anything and anyone who attempted to stand between them.

"She is exquisite, isn't she, brother?"

Kalona moved his gaze from the grove to stare at Erebus. Refusing to speak to him of the Goddess, he said, "Air? Why would you choose such an intangible element to wield?"

Erebus shrugged his sun-kissed shoulders. Kalona noticed that his hair glowed with the same golden fire as did his wings. "My only answer is that which I already gave our Great Mother: it is from the air that we were born. It seemed logical that it should be the element we first command."

"She is not my mother," Kalona said, surprising himself.

Erebus's golden brows raised. "I think our Goddess might disagree with you."

Our Goddess. Kalona hated the sound of those words. "Spend your time thinking of what you will create," Kalona told his brother sharply. "For I assure you, what I create will be worthy of her."

"I do not believe these tests are meant to be a competition," Erebus said.

"Well, brother, I think our Goddess might disagree with you." With those words, Kalona took several strides toward the shoreline. He leaped up at its very edge, beating his wings powerfully and using invisible currents of energy to lift himself.

He could feel Nyx's gaze on him and, just before he disappeared into the horizon, Kalona glanced back. She was standing at the edge of the grove, staring up at him and smiling with a warmth that he could feel against his skin. Kalona met her eyes and touched his lips with his hand. Almost as if they were mirrored beings, Nyx lifted her own hand to touch her lips.

She loves me best! The words in his mind matched the beat of his mighty wings as Kalona climbed into the sky, intent on creating that which would prove he was worthy of his Goddess's favor.

4.

AT THAT MOMENT, KALONA WAS ABSOLUTELY CONTENT…

Kalona didn't think much of the mortal earth. He crossed a great body of water to find a large, fertile continent. But much of it was too hot or too cold. Much of it was uninhabited, and that which was populated by Mother Earth's human children was far from what Kalona's predetermined consciousness considered civilized. He avoided them. Humans might have been created in Nyx's image, but they seemed shallow and uninteresting when compared to the glory of his Goddess. Kalona roamed the vast continent, thinking of Nyx.

He finally came to rest near the center of the continent, drawn down by an expanse of wild grasses that seemed to stretch from below him all the way to the western horizon. He came to ground at the edge of the great prairie, near a sandy stream that rolled musically over smooth river rocks. Kalona drank from the clear, cold water, and then he sat back against the rough bark of a tree.

What could he create from invisible air and Divine power to please Nyx? He searched within and easily found the Divine power that hummed through his blood. Using it, he focused his consciousness outward, and up, far up above the edge of the prairie and the mortal earth. There he found currents of magick, divine trailings of raw and ancient power—the same power that coursed within his blood. Experimenting, Kalona snagged a fragment of ethereal power, pulling it down to him. Then he stood, readying himself, and called, somewhat tentatively, "Air?"

Instantly, the element responded, swirling around him.

"Show me what you can do." Kalona felt foolish, speaking aloud to an invisible element. He pointed at an enormous tree that had somehow grown away from the timberline, proud and alone, well into the tall grasses of the prairie. "With the help of Divine power, I command Air to create that which can be seen from the Otherworld!"

Air rushed around him, capturing the strand of ethereal power, and with a mighty roar, it blew into the tree, which exploded into an enormous mushroom cloud of wood dust and splinters that shot up so far into the sky that Kalona lost sight of it. Large black birds, disturbed in their perches, croaked and circled, chiding him.

The immortal sighed. He did not think that the explosion of a tree, no matter how spectacular, was what—

Kalona's thoughts were interrupted by a sudden influx of power—something that poured into him, as if it were a backwash of energy from the destruction of the tree.

Kalona shook his head, clearing his thoughts. His body tingled briefly, but within seconds the sensation dissipated, leaving him feeling empty and confused. He frowned. He must remember that he was new to this world—new to the powers he had been born to wield. Perhaps he was meant to absorb the remnants of unused energy. Kalona ran his hand through his long, thick hair, speaking his frustration aloud. "How am I to know? It is unfortunate that Mother Earth couldn't allow time for adaptation and understanding before she foisted tests upon me—especially tests that are meant to establish my worth."

Well, he had successfully used Air and the power of the Divine together. And the result probably could have been viewed from the Otherworld, as well as from the sun and the moon. But Kalona didn't believe Nyx would find the sight of splinters and dust and annoyed birds very pleasing. It certainly did not please him as miniscule fragments of the tree began raining down. Kalona was still frowning as he brushed the settling wood dust from his wings. "Air is a ridiculous element," he muttered and then, engulfed in a cloud of wood dust, he coughed and continued brushing dust and shredded leaves from his wings.

"Oh Winged One! Great God! We beg to know your name so that we may worship you and not incur your wrath! Please do not destroy us as you did the Great Spirit Tree!"

Coughing, Kalona looked up from his wings. Squinting through the dust-laden air, he saw a group of natives dressed in leather and feathers and shells prostrating themselves on the opposite bank of the stream. He glanced behind them and stifled a sigh and another cough, tallying one more in his list of mistakes—he'd been so concentrated on the sealike grass prairie and on wielding his power that he hadn't noticed he'd come to ground not far from a human settlement.

Kalona squared his shoulders. Covered in dust or not, he must say *something* to these curious and mistaken children of Mother Earth.

"I am Kalona," he said. They cringed in fear, and he realized he must modulate the power in his voice. He cleared his throat and began anew. "I am Kalona, and I have not come to destroy you."

"Kalona of the Silver Wings, how may we worship you?" asked the human who had first spoken. He was wrinkled and bent but bedecked in more feathers and shells than the others, and his face and bared chest were painted in ocher-colored swirls.

"No, worship is not why I am here," Kalona said.

"But you killed the Great Spirit Tree! You are mightier than it. Now you fill the air with evidence of your power, and the ravens call to you. We plead that you not be like the trickster coyote. We will bring you chigustei and the finest of our boiled meat to eat. The most beautiful of our maidens will warm your bed and dance the Sunrise Dance for you. Just do not destroy us!"

"You do not understand. I am not—"

Kalona's words were cut off as the dust-filled air suddenly cleared and an exquisite woman materialized. She was dressed in the purest of white leathers trimmed in blue stones, round red beads, and carved bone. Her dark hair reached past her slender waist. Her delicate feet were bare, her ankles decorated with ropes of shells so that every time she moved, she made music. Her brown skin was painted with ancient symbols in a blue so dark and rich the design seemed liquid and ever changing. Though in appearance she was totally unlike his first sight of the Goddess, Kalona immediately knew this radiant being was his Nyx.

The humans prostrated themselves again and began to cry, "Estsanatlehi!"

"Beloved Changing Woman!"

"Save us from Kalona of the Silver Wings!"

Kalona coughed once more and then hastily tried to explain, "I did not know it was their tree."

Nyx walked toward him and took his hand, though her attention, and her beautiful dark eyes, were focused entirely on the humans.

"My people, do not fear. Kalona of the Silver Wings is not a destroyer, nor is he a god. He is my—" Nyx paused, flicking her gaze to him. Kalona was sure he saw amusement in her eyes, though she hid her smile well. "My Warrior, my Monster Slayer and my Killer of Enemies," she concluded.

"Did the Great Spirit Tree offend you, Estsanatlehi, so that you sent your Killer of Enemies against it?" asked the feathered, painted man.

"No, Shaman. My Warrior was only making way for a new Great Spirit Tree, one that bears fruit. Behold my gift to you!" Nyx loosed Kalona's hand and turned to face the empty black hole where the tree used to stand. She began moving her bare feet in a dance that had the rhythm of a heartbeat, accompanied by the music of the ropes of shells that decorated her ankles. "Hear me, oh Earth Mother. I am Estsanatlehi, Changing Woman, Speaker for the People. I ask that the Great Spirit Tree be reborn to bear fruit to feed the People. Hear me, oh Earth Mother. I am Estsan-atlehi, Changing Woman, Speaker for the People . . ." Nyx repeated her song over and over, until she had danced around the black hole three full times. With the triple circle completed, she broke off one round red bead from her dress and threw it into the hole with a victorious shout.

Kalona gasped along with the humans when a tree instantly sprouted from the center of the hole, growing up and up, limbs stretching, budding, flowering, then filling out with simple leaves, bright green on the top side and silver on the underside. Kalona blinked, and the entire tree was laden with plump, red fruit.

"Harvest and share this fruit, and remember that your Goddess is not destructive or vengeful," Nyx said, moving back to Kalona's side. "As always, I wish you to blessed be," she concluded. Then she slid her arms up around Kalona's neck and whispered into his ear, "You should take me away from here now."

Hardly able to breathe, Kalona lifted his Goddess into his arms and leaped into the air, holding her tightly as his mighty wings bore them skyward.

"There," Nyx said, pointing down. The land had changed beneath them. It had begun to roll gently and was covered with clusters of tall trees. The Goddess motioned beyond the

trees, toward a wide, dark river dotted with sandbanks and lined with scrub. "You may put me down there."

Kalona circled until he found a gently sloping bank free of weeds and brush. He landed gently.

"You do not have to hold me now," she said. Nyx's head was resting against his shoulder, as it had for most of their journey. He could not see her face, but he could hear the smile in her voice. It gave him courage.

"I like holding you," he said.

"You *are* very strong," she said, laughing softly.

"Does it please you that I am strong?"

"It does when you have to carry me quickly away from a tricky situation."

Kalona did put her down, then, though he stayed close to her, taking both of her hands in his. "Forgive me for that. My intention was not to frighten those mortals. I was— I was trying to . . ." His voice trailed off, and Kalona felt his face flame in embarrassment.

Nyx smiled and cupped his cheek with her soft hand. "You were trying to what?"

"Please you!" he said in a rush of honesty.

"You thought destroying a tree would please me?"

He shook his head and tree dust fell from his hair into her face. Nyx sneezed violently three times and rubbed at her watering eyes.

"Forgive me again!" He lifted his hands impotently, trying to help her, and as if it had just been waiting for that movement of his hands, more dust rained from his arms onto her face. She sneezed again and, unable to speak, motioned for him to step back. Frustration blazed through him, attracting wisps of Divine power. With a sudden idea, Kalona blurted, "Air, help create a soothing peace for Nyx!"

He held his breath while air whirled around his Goddess, carrying the luminous fragments of his power so that they gently brushed against her skin, blowing the dust from her face and leaving her blinking away the last of her tears and smiling at him.

"Now, *that* pleased me. Thank you, Kalona."

"Then you forgive me for the tree? And frightening those humans? And the dust?"

"Of course I do. You meant no harm with any of it. Though I still do not understand what you intended to create back there."

"Something you could view from the Otherworld," Kalona said. Then he added, "My invocation was flawed, my intent muddled. I am not sure what I expected to happen, but I am sure I failed."

"Oh, I wouldn't say it was a total failure. You did get my attention, though it was because I felt the fear of the People."

"Truly, I meant them no harm," he said.

"I believe you, but I must also tell you what Mother Earth did not fully explain to you or Erebus. Many of her humans are childlike in their beliefs. They are easily frightened and tell elaborate stories to make sense of that which they cannot fully understand. However, I am especially fond of the race of mortals you met today. They have a deep love and respect for the earth, and a loyalty that touches my heart. I probably appear to them more than I should, but I do enjoy the stories they tell about me."

"Is that why you look like this today? Because they wouldn't recognize you if they saw you as you were earlier?"

"Yes, partially. I find the different races of humanity are more comfortable if I appear to them looking as much like them as possible." Nyx smiled, suddenly girlish again. "And I enjoy taking on different visages. I find beauty in all of them. Just as I find beauty in so much of the earth and the mortals who inhabit it." She gestured at the wide, sandy river. "I love the water of this world, everything from rivers like this, to the great lakes that are north of here, and the sapphire and turquoise oceans that separate continents. Their beauty intrigues me. There is one lake in the northwest of this land that is so blue and deep and cold that it dazzles me each time I visit it."

"Are there no bodies of water in the Otherworld?"

"Of course! But not like here—not as deep and mysterious and seemingly endless. *And* here they are not filled with merefolk and naiads. The Fey rarely allow me to enjoy the tranquillity of floating, free of worries and responsibilities, on a cool, clear lake." Her expression was dreamy and she swayed toward him. "May I tell you a secret?"

"You may tell me many secrets. I would guard them for eternity."

"I believe you would. Thank you for that," she said, and leaned forward, kissing him chastely on the cheek. "My secret is that sometimes I alter my appearance and visit earth, pretending to be mortal. I sit and gaze out across a lake or a river or an ocean, and I dream."

"Of what do you dream, Goddess?" Kalona asked, the skin of his cheek still tingling from her kiss.

"I dream of love and happiness and peace. I dream that there is no Darkness in this world or in mine. I dream that mortals would stop struggling against one another and unite instead. And I dream that I am not eternally alone."

"But you are a Goddess, immortal, divine, and powerful. Could you not force the mortals to be peaceful, to shun Darkness?"

Nyx's smile was sad. "I could if I wanted to take free will from them. I wouldn't like that, though. And I promise you, they wouldn't, either. And I am beginning to understand that even the absence of strife would not rid this world or mine of Darkness."

"Explain this Darkness of which you speak," Kalona said.

"I don't think I can—or at least not well. I am inexperienced with it. So far I have only sensed its malevolence and witnessed what those under its influence will do. Humans can be very cruel when incited. Did you know that?"

Kalona did not, but he realized he did not because he had not been paying much attention to the mortals that inhabited earth. His only focus had been on winning his place at Nyx's side. He was just beginning to understand he might need to be by her side for more reasons than the desire he felt for her.

"Are you in danger, Nyx?"

The Goddess met his gaze. "I do not know."

"These ridiculous tests! They keep me from you. I should be beside you, protecting you!"

She studied him carefully, not reacting to his outburst. Eventually he felt foolish, and he stared out at the lazily flowing river.

"You are eager to speak about human strife and the dangers of Darkness. You are quick to leap to my defense."

"Always!" he assured her, wondering why she suddenly looked so sad.

"But you say nothing of my eternal loneliness."

"I thought I need say nothing—that you understood that if I was your protector, I would be by your side, your lover and mate, eternally watching over you."

"Kalona, perhaps a good lesson for you to learn is to never presume you know what a Goddess, or any woman, is thinking," Nyx said. With a smile she motioned for him to join her as she settled on a smooth driftwood log and began to pick through the pebbles by her bare feet, choosing some and discarding others.

Kalona sat and, not knowing what to say next, blurted, "Is earth really like the Otherworld?"

"Yes and no," she explained. "The earth is to the Otherworld as the People's Great Spirit Tree is to a Goddess."

"Then the earth is only a wan reflection of the Otherworld," Kalona said, unable to keep the relief from his voice.

Nyx's gaze flicked up to meet his briefly before she went back to choosing rocks. She continued, "Though only a reflection of the Otherworld, there is a unique beauty on earth that is made even more special and precious because nothing remains the same here. Humanity lives and dies and then lives again. The seasons change. The continents shift. Human life happens here, love happens here, birth and death happen here. Humanity's time is brief but fascinating and heartbreaking and exquisite. I hope that someday you will come to value humans, and the earth, as I do."

"I value you, above all things," Kalona said.

Nyx met his gaze. "I know you do. I could feel our connection when first I looked into your amber eyes. Since then I believe you have intoxicated me."

Kalona went to his knees before her. "Tell me what I can create that would please you most! I want only to make you happy and to be by your side always as your protector and mate."

"Kalona, son of the Mighty Moon I love so well, I cannot tell you what to create for me. That would be unfair to my friend, Mother Earth. It is she who is responsible for you coming into being. It is she who has devised the tests you must endure. I cannot, will not, usurp her responsibilities. What I can tell you is that I wish only for you to be yourself—strong, honest, and unique—in these tests, and during the eternity I hope we might share together." She took his hand then and stood, pulling him up with her. "Now I'd like to share something with you about this world, this changing, funny, fabulous world. Come with me!"

As lithe as a maiden, Nyx skipped away toward the sandy edge of the riverbank. Willingly, Kalona followed the music of shells she left in her wake. They reached the riverbank, and Kalona noticed she was holding up the skirt of her buckskin dress so that a pouch had been created in which she carried a pile of stones she had chosen.

"This is what you do. You pick a rock, the smoother, rounder, and flatter the better. Then you throw it thus!" With a deft flick of her wrist, the Goddess let loose a rock, tossing it into the slowly moving river.

Kalona laughed aloud in surprise as her stone didn't sink. Instead it skipped over the top of the water, as gracefully as Nyx had skipped to the edge of the bank. Then the Goddess jumped up and down in happiness. "Five times! It skipped five times! That one was special. Here, you try."

Hesitantly, Kalona chose a rock, hoping it was smooth and round and flat enough. He furrowed his brow in concentration. He tried to aim. He flicked his wrist several times in practice, not letting the rock go yet, intent on getting it as perfect as possible.

"Kalona."

Nyx's voice was soft. He turned to her questioningly.

She leaned into him, lifted up onto her bare toes, and kissed him gently, gently on his lips. His arms went around her and he drank in the unique scent of her skin. What was it? Something sweet and something earthy that drew him to her and made him want nothing more than to be close to her forever. "This is fun, not a test," she whispered. "Relax, mighty Killer of my Enemies. I believe you can be playmate *and* warrior." Obviously reluctant to leave his arms, she pulled free slowly, letting her hand linger on his chest. "Now, have fun!" she said, shoving him backward so that his wings had to unfurl to keep him from falling on his firm behind.

Nyx giggled, then clamped her hand over her mouth and giggled some more.

Kalona thought her laughter was as infectious as her scent was alluring. He righted himself, strode to the edge of the water, and without aiming at all, tossed the rock into the river, where it landed with a liquid *plop* and sank immediately.

He looked at Nyx, who was trying, unsuccessfully, to stifle more giggles. "Well," he said with mock seriousness. "It appears that unlike you, I can only do one thing well at a time."

Nyx swallowed another giggle and cocked her head at him. "What one thing are you doing well?"

"I am being intoxicating," he said, and reached up to brush a patch of lingering wood dust from his chest.

Nyx's dark eyes were alight with humor. She grinned at him and said, "Good. Then I will continue to beat you in stone skipping and anything else I put my mind to." The Goddess flicked another rock over the surface of the river and shouted in triumph when it skipped six times before disappearing beneath the surface.

Kalona rubbed his chin. "Perhaps I should work on being less intoxicating."

Nyx smiled at him. "Please don't. I prefer you just as you are."

"So you have spoken. So mote it be." Kalona caressed

her cheek gently with the back of his hand before snatching a flat stone from her pile and flicking it into the river, where it skipped three times before sinking.

Nyx's cheers joined his and, laughing, Kalona began skipping rocks, one after another, side by side with his Goddess.

At that moment, Kalona was absolutely content.

5.

I MISS YOU THE INSTANT I AM NOT IN YOUR PRESENCE...

"I know I am favoring Kalona," Nyx said, staring into the mirror of her looking glass as L'ota combed out her silver-blond hair and began braiding it in an impossibly intricate pattern. "I don't mean to. It isn't as if I dislike Erebus. On the contrary! Every time I see Erebus he makes me laugh. He is so clever and talented. Did you know he can sing and play the lyre? Actually, it was his voice that yesterday drew me from the Otherworld to Greece. He was playing and singing so beautifully that all of Delos had named him winged Apollo Incarnate. They were placing olive branches at his feet and worshipping him."

Not to be worshipped. The skeeaed whispered disapprovingly.

"Oh, no, he didn't allow them to worship him. Even before he knew I was part of the watching crowd he laughed at being called a God and made a big show of missing notes, pretending that he was a traveling musician—and not a very good one at that—and that his wings were part of his costume. With a sleight of hand too swift for mortal eyes to follow, he called Air and mixed it with Divine

Energy, and suddenly he was wearing a mask that made him look like a silly bird. Within moments he had the audience laughing and following him in a preening dance, and utterly forgetting how godlike he truly is." Nyx smiled as she remembered how sweet and silly Erebus had made himself look, just for the benefit of the watching mortals.

She wondered if Kalona would have done the same had she not appeared to intercede between him and the people of the prairie. Her smile faded. He had been denying his godhood, hadn't he?

You think of the other one, L'ota said.

"I do. I think of him often. Something happened when I first looked into his eyes—something wonderful."

Must be worthy of you, the skeeaed said, her whispering voice sounding unusually forceful.

Nyx gave her a curious look. "L'ota, they both were created for me—Erebus *and* Kalona. Mother Earth's tests are but a formality. She is, after all, acting as mother, which means she is being fondly, but predictably, over-protective."

The skeeaed didn't meet her Goddess's gaze in the looking glass, and Nyx shrugged her shoulders. "No matter. I do not expect you to understand, little L'ota. Erebus and Kalona are not your concern. Now, where are the dryads I summoned?" Nyx stood and walked to the wall of windows that overlooked the exquisite grounds of her palace, not noticing that the skeeaed had gone silent and sulky at the Goddess's dismissive words. "I asked a group of dryads to gather gardenias from the mortal realm so that you might weave them into my hair. Have you noticed that since I allowed them to visit the earth, the dryads always seem distracted?"

Only notice what you command to notice, L'ota murmured too softly for Nyx to hear.

The Goddess had turned from the window to glance at the skeeaed when her chamber exploded in a flurry of trilling dryads whose arms were filled with fragrant white flowers, shifting to and from dizzying shades of greens and blues and purples in their excitement.

"What are you—" Nyx stopped, realizing what must have caused the Feys' excitement. "One of them is ready to begin his test!"

The Fey leaped and danced around her, dropping gardenias into her hair, and causing L'ota to scold them as she hastily rearranged her Goddess's braids.

"Which one is it?" Nyx asked breathlessly, forcing herself to sit still so L'ota could finish her toilette and the overly enlivened dryads could quickly drape her body in the robes she'd chosen, which were the color of a maiden's blush.

The dryads began trilling again and Nyx shook her head in consternation. They were too excited. Not even the Goddess could understand their high-pitched chatter.

L'ota understood her kin perfectly. She whispered one word to the Goddess: *Kalona.*

Nyx had no trouble finding Kalona. Over the passing days since his creation, she had learned that all she need do was to think of him—to picture his strong, handsome face in her mind—and she would be drawn to him.

She had tried finding Erebus the same way and had been unsuccessful. Nyx spoke of this failure to no one, especially not to Kalona or Erebus.

That day, the picture in her mind took her back to a familiar place—the grass-filled prairie not far from where Kalona had exploded the Great Spirit Tree. Though, she noted as she smiled and hurried to greet Mother Earth, this time he was not so close to the mortal settlement.

"One of your godlings has declared he is ready to be tested," Mother Earth said after embracing Nyx. Then she smiled happily. "Ah! You have brought the Fey with you! I have so been enjoying their company."

Nyx gave the frolicking Fey an indulgent smile. "You spoil them."

"They are delightful! I enjoy spoiling them," Mother Earth said, petting one of the trilling dryads fondly. "Oh! This is a new Fey!" she said, spotting L'ota. "What are you, beautiful one?"

"L'ota is a skeeaed. One that serves me personally."

"She is lovely," Mother Earth said, and then shared a

smile with L'ota. "Please visit me often, and bring more of your kind with you."

If Nyx allows . . .

"She does speak! How interesting."

"Of course I allow, L'ota. You and the rest of the skee-aeds may visit Mother Earth whenever your duties allow," Nyx said absently, searching the skies for Kalona.

"He is not here yet, though he did have Air summon me. Your Kalona should be taught Goddesses do not like to be kept waiting."

Suddenly a flock of ravens as dark as a new moon sky circled above them and then perched as if watching in the nearby trees.

"Nyx! I have missed you." Kalona dropped from the sky above them to kneel before his Goddess.

Her breath caught at his raw beauty. He was wearing elaborately stitched and fringed leather pants that had been dyed to match the white of his wings. His chest was bare, though swirls of ocher decorated its muscular expanse. She thought he looked like he could be a mighty God Warrior of the Prairie People. Eagerly, she took his hand, pulling him to his feet, flirting playfully.

"Missed me? But I spent much of last night with you climbing the boughs of the giant trees near the ocean and gazing out at the moonlit water." She turned his hand so that it was palm up. "See, you still bear the stains of the sweet berries you harvested for me. How could you possibly miss me in less than one day?"

"I miss you the instant I am not in your presence."

Kalona words were not teasing, and his amber gaze held Nyx's while he gently stroked her cheek with the back of his hand.

Mother Earth cleared her throat delicately. "You did summon me here because you were ready to unveil your creation, did you not, Kalona?"

"I did," Kalona said. Without any more hesitation, he moved several long strides away from them. He faced the two women and the flock of Fey who hovered around them. "Nyx, I create for you something that demonstrates the power of the passion I will eternally feel for you."

Kalona lifted his arms, unfurling his great moonlight-colored wings. His voice, filled with the ancient power of the Divine, intensified by Air, echoed across the grasslands.

> *Winds of force, I do call thee forth!*
> *Through my blood, I do summon power!*
> *Strength of passion, I do command you show!*
> *Creation of mine, the Goddess Nyx to know!*

With a deafening *crack!* Kalona clapped his mighty hands together, and instantly the air above them began to roil and blow, around and around, so that great thunderclouds billowed and the sky went from sweet summer's day blue to bruised and angry and dark.

> *Now grow! Grow! Far afield grow!*
> *Creation of mine, the Goddess Nyx to know!*

With the repetition of his words, Kalona also repeated the thunderclap of his hands, and the swirling winds above him shot into the distance. As the winds moved they changed, alight with shards of spearlike power, they roared, forming a vortex that became a funnel, which dipped down, down, until its gray tail met the prairie in an explosion of one element clashing with another. The funnel skipped across the grasslands, leaving a trail of destruction in its wake.

Nyx forced her gaze from Kalona's terrible, wondrous creation to look at him. Kalona blazed. He stood in the center of a maelstrom of wind and power, staring at her with a desire so powerful it frightened her. The Goddess could not speak. She was trapped in his gaze, drawn and repelled, equally as afraid of losing him as of accepting him.

"Control it, you fool!" Mother Earth shouted her command over the wind. "It has changed course!"

Nyx looked to where the funnel had been only moments ago. It was gone! She searched the sky and realized it had skipped across the flat ground of the prairie, changed direction, and was heading toward the timberline, which held the settlement of the People.

"Air! I command you depart!" Kalona cried.

But Kalona's task was complete, and he no longer commanded Air. The whipping winds within the funnel howled and grew, bearing down on the campsite.

From the sky there was a flash of gold and Erebus dropped to the ground, standing tall and proud between the whirlwind and the tree line. In a strong, sure voice he commanded:

> *Winds of storm and lightning, passion and power,*
> *I command thee with a different intent.*
> *Peace and calm I do bring to this hour.*
> *Now! My creation to the Goddess I present!"*

Erebus clapped his hands together, and sunlight burst from his palms, spearing into the heart of the dark, whirling funnel cloud. Like dew scorched by summer sun rays, the clouds parted, dissolving the passion of the storm. From the very center of what had so recently been a spiral of chaotic passion and power, color grew and arched, spreading in a brilliant bow of yellow and pink, crimson, purple, and green.

The dryads, who had been cringing in fear, hiding down in the tall grass, crept out, cooing and trilling in appreciation of the colorful show. Even L'ota, who had been cowering behind Nyx, peeked out and gasped in pleasure.

"Do you like it?" Erebus asked, jogging up to Nyx and bowing first to her and then to Mother Earth. "I was a little rushed. I had planned to present it for you at dusk today, when the colors would look most brilliant, but I was drawn here by that maelstrom, and knew my plans must change." Erebus frowned at Kalona. "What were you thinking?"

"I was *not* thinking about you!"

Nyx's eyes widened in surprise at Kalona's harsh tone, but before she could admonish him, Mother Earth spoke.

"You were not thinking about anyone except yourself! Kalona, you have failed this test." Her displeasure caused the prairie grasses to shiver. Mother Earth turned her back on Kalona and went to Erebus, embracing him warmly. "Erebus, your creation is lovely, and I thank you for ending the terrible storm that could have destroyed some of my children."

"Wait, my friend." Nyx addressed Mother Earth slowly, carefully considering each of her words. "When you commanded that Kalona and Erebus complete three tasks, you proclaimed that as their Goddess, it is my right to judge their creations. I would respectfully remind you of your own proclamation."

Mother Earth met Nyx's gaze. The Goddess searched for anger or resentment within her friend's eyes, but she saw only concern, and then resignation. Mother Earth bowed her head to Nyx. "You do well to remind me of my words. I bow to your judgment."

Drawing a deep breath, Nyx faced Kalona. He had moved toward her as the funnel had gotten out of control, and she knew he had been ready to protect her against his own creation. She also knew the misery she saw in his amber eyes. She felt the mirrored pain within herself.

"Kalona, what you created for me did exactly as you intended. It demonstrated the power of your passion, and I could view your whirlwind from the Otherworld. I appreciate your strength and your desire to share your innermost passions with me. You do wield the power of an immortal warrior, *my* immortal warrior, and that pleases me. But if you are ever to be more than warrior to me, you must temper your passion with kindness, your power with control." She closed the space between them. She needed to touch him. To let him hold her in his arms as he had the night before as he had fed her berries and gazed at the moonlit ocean with her. But for his own sake, Nyx denied her need and finished her judgment. "I understand the intent behind your creation, and because of that you did not fail the test, but you did not please me, either."

Kalona's shoulders drooped and he did not meet her eyes. "I ask that you forgive me and give me another chance to please you, for I desire to be much more than your Warrior."

"Readily, I forgive you and grant you another chance. Which element would you choose to wield?"

His gaze found hers again. "The one that is so favored by you—Water."

"My friend?" Nyx said, looking from Kalona to Mother Earth.

Mother Earth nodded and said, "Until you each call into being your creation, I grant you dominion over Water. So I have spoken; so mote it be."

"Thank you, Mother Earth," Nyx said. Without another word to Kalona, Nyx turned her back to him and walked to Erebus. Embracing him warmly, she said, "Erebus, your bow of color is lovely! You have pleased me greatly. Would you walk awhile with me? I would like to introduce you to the People of the Prairie. After what they have witnessed today, I am sure your music would bring them much needed delight."

"Goddess, it is my greatest pleasure to do your bidding."

Nyx let him take her hand and together they walked through the grasses toward the timberline. Though she wanted to, the Goddess did not allow herself to look back at Kalona even once.

6.

TRUST ME, GODDESS. I WOULD NEVER LET YOU FALL...

Kalona sulked for several days after the test, replaying over and over again in his mind the disastrous conclusion to what he had intended as an awe-inspiring demonstration of passion and power.

How had it gone so terribly wrong?

He had practiced day after day on the grassy prairie. The neighboring tribe of Prairie People could have attested to the fact that he had created many whirling funnels of wind and magick, and that he had easily controlled them. The local mortals had even begun leaving gifts of food, clay pots filled with precious ocher, and carefully made clothing for him. Remembering Nyx's fondness for these particular people, Kalona had dressed carefully for his test, decorating himself to please her.

But nothing had gone as Kalona had planned.

Erebus had saved the day *and* won Nyx's pleasure. Kalona could not bear to think of what else Erebus had won from Nyx.

He would not allow himself to fail again!

"It is that wretched elemental magick that was at fault.

Air is so unpredictable—so changeable. It was Erebus's choice in elements that was flawed. Though is my choice of Water any better?" He paced around the clearing he had begun to think of as his own. It was far enough from the tribe of Prairie People that they did not often pass by, and close enough that the offerings they had continued to leave for him were easily accessible. The People did not particularly interest Kalona, but their food did, as did the thick, soft furs they'd left for his sleeping pallet. Not surprisingly, Mother Earth's surface was as hard and uncomfortable as her admonishing gaze. The immortal had no true need for sleep, though that did not mean he didn't appreciate a warm, soft spot on which to rest his body.

"Cro-oak! Cro-oak! Cro-oak!" Above Kalona, the ravens that had taken to following him around the prairie lent their words to his tirade.

"If you must shadow me, do it quietly!"

The black birds preened and stared at him. Kalona shook his head. "I have to find my focus! I must wield Water more wisely than I did Air. I must win Nyx's pleasure from Erebus."

That shouldn't have been so difficult. Before the botched test, Nyx had regularly sought him out. They had spent many days and nights together, and she had seemed well pleased to be in his presence.

"Without being wooed by an unpredictable element!" Kalona shouted his frustration, causing the ravens to flutter their wings restlessly.

Kalona stopped pacing and reasoned aloud. "I pleased her without using an element or invoking Divine magick to do so. I did it before, and I shall do it again. And from an intimate, pleasant interlude wherein I remind her that it is *me* she desires, not magick or elements or the unpredictable power of creation, I will take her to my next test. It will be something as simple and intimate as our interlude, and I will be victorious, winning Nyx's favor!" Kalona hurried to the pile of furs and leathers and such that were rich gifts from the Prairie People. He dug through the mound until he found what he sought—a knife made of a black stone, hewn to a strong, sharp point. "I am liking these Prairie People more and more each day." Kalona rolled the knife and a basket of fruit and fragrant flatbread within the softest of the furs, and then he took to the sky and headed into the northwest, seeking that which he knew would please his Goddess.

He didn't use magick to fell the tall pine tree, though he did use his immortal strength, as well as his preternatural speed, to hollow it out and carve from it the form of a gracefully pointed boat. Kalona found he enjoyed using his hands as much as he enjoyed the scent of wood and the sight of the azure lake. Nyx had been right about the beauty of the lake. Its color was so lovely that he often glanced at it to be sure it wasn't just a trick of his sight. But it didn't change. Even under the moonlight the huge round body of water, dotted with one tree-covered island, seemed to glisten aqua, its high sides looking like a bowl made of clouds that had trapped the sky.

Kalona worked without pause all day and night on the little boat, and as he worked he thought of Nyx. Her beauty inspired him, and when he was finished he stood back and surveyed his work. Kalona was well pleased. The craft was more than seaworthy. Kalona liked to believe that it also reflected Nyx's beauty. All around it he had meticulously carved symbols that reminded him of the Goddess: stars and moons, delicate shells and waves. He had even replicated the white flowers she had worn in her hair when last he'd seen her.

He carried the boat down the steep side of the lake so that it rested on the rocky shore. Then he placed the thick, soft fur within it, as well as the basket of fruit and flatbread. He was ready for Nyx. He had even decided what he would create for her during his next test. He hadn't practiced over and over again as he had with the funnel cloud, but he felt confident that he had changed his intent enough that he wouldn't make the same mistake as before. This time he would not show her the power of his passion. This time he would make tangible the delight he felt at her beauty, and show her how much he cherished her, in whatever visage she chose.

There was just one thing that he couldn't figure out, and that was how to get Nyx to come to him without using Water to summon meddling Mother Earth. He wanted to be alone with his Goddess before the test, to show her what his own hands had created for her before he wielded magick and Water and put on the requisite public show.

Kalona had never had to call Nyx to him before. She had just appeared, usually smiling and telling him to stop looking so serious and come gather flowers with her, or gaze at moonlit water with her, or kiss her, gently, just where her impossibly soft skin curved to meet her graceful shoulders . . .

Kalona shook himself mentally. *Thinking* of kissing Nyx would not conjure the Goddess.

Perhaps he should try calling her name.

"Nyx?" His voice echoed back to him over the brilliant blue surface of the lake, sounding tentative and almost childlike. Kalona squared his shoulders and tried again. "Nyx!" This time the echo was more forceful, though it produced the same result. Nyx did not appear.

"Think!" he commanded himself. "There must be a way to reach her without using Mother Earth's element and bringing the whole crowd of them here."

As if his words had conjured a small part of that crowd, the little creature stepped from behind a nearby pine tree and spoke mockingly in its whispery voice, *Goddess not called like servant! Goddess commands, not commanded!*

"You are one of Nyx's Fey. I saw you beside her on the prairie."

As soon as Kalona spoke, the Fey skittered back behind the tree.

"Don't run away! I need your help." Kalona pitched his voice to sound coaxing, soothing. The creature, moving with an odd, liquid grace, slid part of its body from behind the tree, peeking out at him. "Don't be frightened. I will not harm you."

Not frightened, said the Fey, moving all the way out from behind the tree.

"That's right, you don't need to be frightened of me."

L'ota not frightened.

"L'ota? Is that the type of Fey you are?"

The creature looked thoroughly offended. *I skeeaed! Servant of Goddess! She name me.*

"So, you *are* close to Nyx."

Always.

Kalona hid his smile. "If you are always close to Nyx, then where is she? I do not see her."

L'ota's strangely shaped body rippled in consternation, changing colors from pale pink to crimson and rust. *Not here. Otherworld.*

Kalona couldn't contain his smile. "Are you here watching me for her?"

No! L'ota exclaimed, her voice rising above its usual whisper.

Kalona's smiled faded. "She didn't send you to watch me?"

I watch for me, not for Goddess.

Kalona's brows lifted in amusement. "Why would you want to watch me?"

You make Goddess sad. I want know why.

Kalona felt as if the strange little Fey had driven a knife into his heart. "Nyx has been sad?"

The creature's elongated head nodded, making the pink fringe of fur on its head bob. *I want know why.*

Kalona thought the creature didn't sound particularly worried about Nyx, or even concerned that her Goddess was sad. It just sounded curious.

"I want to know why, too. And I want to make sure she is never sad because of me again. The only way I can do that is to have her come here to me, so that I can fix the wrong I did that saddened her. L'ota, please go to your Goddess and tell her that I ask—no, that I entreat—she come to me."

The Fey went very still, and Kalona held his breath, waiting. When she finally spoke, L'ota surprised Kalona with her nonchalance.

If you command I tell Goddess you here.

"If I command you? That's all it takes to get you to tell Nyx I'm here and that I entreat she come to me?"

No matter. Not my concern. Only notice what commanded to notice.

Kalona thought the creature thoroughly odd, but he said, "Then I command that you go to Nyx and entreat her to come to me."

L'ota's body completely liquefied and she disappeared, leaving Kalona to stare after her and worry that he had, again, made a mistake.

"You found my favorite lake."

Her voice startled him. He'd been sitting on a rock,

staring out at the blue water. So much time had passed since the strange little skeeaed had disappeared that he had begun to despair of Nyx coming. The sound of her voice was like balm on the aching wound that was his heart. He stood and turned so quickly that he almost lost his balance.

She smiled. "Hello."

"Hello," he said. He took in every detail of his Goddess. Today she had chosen to appear to him as the young maiden she had been when they'd first met. Her blond hair curled down past her shoulders. Her dress was simple, the color of the summer sky—the color of her eyes. The only adornment she wore was her mantle of stars, which rested over her hair like a headdress made of silver strung diamonds and the fascinating sapphire tattoos that decorated her skin.

Nyx was the most beautiful thing Kalona had ever seen, and he knew he could spend an eternity gazing into her eyes.

"I have missed you." They spoke the words together.

Kalona could contain himself no longer. His long strides closed the space between them and he gently, carefully, took her into his arms and just stood, holding her, breathing in her scent as every particle of his being rejoiced.

"Yes," he said, nuzzling her hair and whispering into her ear. "I found your favorite lake."

She pulled back a little so that she could smile up into his eyes. "I am glad you called for me."

"I am glad you came." He returned her smile. It frightened him how her presence could make him so happy, and how her absence could make him so miserable, but he pushed aside those thoughts, determined to stay in the moment, to enjoy every instant he had alone with her. "I made you something."

Her smile dimmed. "Oh. You're ready to complete the next test? We must call—"

He touched her lips with his finger, silencing her gently. "I am ready to complete the next test, but first I want to show you what I *made* for you. I didn't use magick. I didn't call Water. I only used my desire to please you. I need no test to school me in that." Putting his arm around her shoulders, he guided her to the spot where he had beached the boat.

He felt her little start of surprise. "You made this for me?"

"I did."

She pulled free from his half embrace and hurried to the boat, running her hands over the symbols carved around it and making soft sounds of delight. When she looked up at him, her eyes were filled with tears.

"I wanted you to be able to float on the lake in peace and to think of nothing but the beauty that surrounds you," he said. "I hope it pleases you."

Nyx rushed to him and, laughing, hurled herself into his arms. Clinging to his neck, she covered his face in kisses, between kisses saying, "Yes, it pleases me! I love it! Thank you! Thank you!"

He was laughing with her as he spread his wings and

lifted her from the ground, twirling her around. Neither realized they were hovering in the air until Nyx's gaze tried to find the boat. She gasped and clutched his neck. Kalona tightened his arms around her.

"Trust me, Goddess. I would never let you fall."

Nyx gazed into his eyes. "I trust you." Then she kissed him. Not playfully, or gently, as she had before. The Goddess kissed him as if she thirsted, and only he could slake her need.

Kalona responded to her passion carefully. He wanted to crush her to him and to claim her as his own. But even more than that, he wanted to please her. So, he let Nyx take her time exploring his lips, touching his face, combing her fingers through his long, thick hair. All the while he held her. He kept her safe.

Too soon she paused her exploration, though the flush of her face and the deepening of her breath told him she had enjoyed herself as surely as her words did. "I like the way you taste," she said.

He smiled, glad that he had tempered his desire with patience. "And *that*, my Goddess, pleases me."

"Would you take me out in your boat?"

"It would be my pleasure, but it isn't my boat. It is yours."

"Kalona, sometimes you say exactly the right thing."

He snorted as they drifted slowly to ground. "Sometimes, but not often."

"I think you're getting better at it," she said.

"I could not get much worse." Taking her hand, he helped her into the boat. "I-I made a mess of the Air test," he said, pushing the craft out into the water before he got in with her. When she didn't answer him, he made himself keep busy with the wooden paddle, steering the boat out onto the glasslike surface of the lake.

When he finally looked at her, Nyx was watching him, her expression unreadable.

"You are still angry with me?" he asked.

She shook her head. "I was never angry with you. I was sad and disappointed."

"Knowing I have caused you sadness wounds me," he said. "I will do better with the next test. I vow it."

"It wasn't the test that made me sad. It wasn't the test that disappointed me."

"What then?"

"You were cruel to Erebus. He did not deserve that."

Kalona almost snapped the paddle in two. Unable to contain his jealousy, he blurted, "You do not prefer him!"

"Kalona, you *both* were created for me. You *both* have a purpose and a place at my side. If you do not want to sadden or disappoint me, you will not harbor enmity for your brother."

Kalona struggled to control his inner turmoil. He wanted to cry out, to tell her that he couldn't bear to share her, couldn't bear to think of her covering Erebus's face with joyous kisses, or exploring the taste of his lips.

"I vow that I have love enough within me for the both of you," she said, moving forward so that she could press the palm of her hand over his heart. "Trust me, Kalona. I will never break a vow." Then she kissed him and Kalona could think of nothing but the scent of her skin and the wonder of her touch.

The waters around them exploded with trilling Fey. They leaped over and around the boat in agitation, calling frantically to Nyx.

"Yes, yes, I understand you. I know the place. I will come. I will come." The Goddess told the creatures, and with satisfied chirps, they disappeared as quickly as they had appeared. Nyx sighed and wiped water from her face and his, smiling apologetically at him.

"Let me guess," Kalona said. "Erebus is ready for his test."

"You are correct," she said. "May we continue what we began later?"

"Yes, of course," he said, turning the boat toward shore, hiding his hurt and frustration from her.

He helped her from the boat, pulling it well up onto the rocky shore. He was silent, already anticipating the joy Nyx would feel at whatever magnificent show Erebus had concocted for her this time, when the Goddess circled him with her arms from behind, pressing her cheek against his bare back and nuzzling his silver wings.

"I wish you would choose happiness. There is such wondrous happiness between us—enough to last an eternity," she said.

He pressed his arms over hers, loving the feel of her warmth against the moonlit coolness of his skin. He drew a deep breath, and with it made a conscious effort to release his frustration.

Kalona could feel her smile. "There! That's better," she said, and kissed first the middle of his back, and then each of his wings. He thought she would release him then, though he remained very still, hoping to gain even one more small moment with her. She took her arms from around him, but she remained close. He sensed her hesitation, and then she stroked each of his wings gently. "They are so beautiful. I could look at them forever and still find different colors within them. Did you know that they're not really white?"

"They are behind me, thus difficult for me to see." His smile was reflected in his voice.

"They are like moonlight, of course, but this close their color reminds me of pearls. So beautiful . . ." she repeated, stroking them.

Kalona turned and caught her in his arms. "That you can find such beauty in me is a special kind of magick."

"All is well between us," she said, staring into his eyes searchingly. "Please know that. Your place in my heart cannot be filled by any other being in this realm or the Otherworld."

Kalona kissed her gently. "Tell me, Goddess, where shall I take you?"

"To the east, and then a little north. If I understood the naiads correctly, which sometimes takes some doing, Erebus has chosen a fragrant spot for the site of his next test."

Kalona couldn't help grumbling. "What is he going to do? Water a field of flowers for you?"

Nyx laughed and twined her arms around his neck. "That isn't exactly the fragrance I recall from this place, so creating flowers there would, truly, be an exceptional thing."

Kalona took to the air with his Goddess in his embrace, dreading what was to come.

7.

YOUR BROTHERHOOD PLEASES ME MORE THAN ANY TEST EVER COULD…

"Argh! It is putrid!" Kalona's nose was wrinkled in disgust. "I will not take you closer to that mud and mess."

"Nyx, there you are! It is lovely to see you." Mother Earth embraced her.

"It is a pleasure to see you, as well." Nyx returned her embrace, and then smiled at the dancing dryads that had taken to following the Great Mother everywhere. "If ever I wonder where they have gotten off to, I know all I need do is find you, and there the Fey will be."

Mother Earth's gaze went to Kalona. "And if ever I wonder where you have gotten off to, I know all I need do is find Kalona, and there Nyx will be."

Kalona bowed his head slightly but respectfully to her. "I greet you, Earth Mother."

"I greet you as well," she said. "Whenever you are ready, you may begin your test. I do hope it turns out better than your last one."

"I am ready, but—"

"But it is me who has summoned you here! There is no need for you to move from this spot. From here you will have a perfect view." Erebus dropped down from the sky above them, glistening as golden as the midday sun. "Mother Earth, your beauty outshines the majesty of the pine trees," he said with a flourish and a bow.

"So charming and handsome." Mother Earth smiled fondly at him.

Then he turned to Nyx, and from behind his back he produced a single length of a fragrant herb, topped with a brilliant purple flower. Moving to her, he smiled and said, "Hello, my Goddess. This plant reminded me of the scent of your skin. I hope my creation pleases you as much as it does me." Erebus tucked the sprig in her hair behind her ear.

Nyx smiled. "Lavender! You are right, Erebus. I do so love its delicate fragrance. I often rub it on my wrists. Thank you."

"You should have brought enough for all of us so that we could stand the stench of this place," Kalona said gruffly.

"Brother, I have actually missed your scowling face, but probably only because it bears such a resemblance to my own!" He clapped Kalona on the shoulder.

Nyx thought Kalona's face looked like a thundercloud ready to explode all over his brother.

"There is nothing wrong with the scent of this place," Mother Earth said sternly. "It comes from the mixing of heat and minerals that rest just below ground. During the winter, many animals come here and take comfort in the warmth it provides. They do not complain of the smell, and neither would you, Kalona, were you to freeze to death otherwise."

"I am an immortal. We never die," Kalona told her placidly.

"Indeed?" Mother Earth replied. "Never is a very long time."

"Then let us waste not another moment of it," Nyx said. "Erebus, what is it you have created for me with Water and magick?"

"Hopefully, something that pleases you greatly." With two beats of his great golden wings, Erebus took to the air, hovering above them, near the lip of the basin that held mud and fetid escaping vapor.

> *Mud and heat from earth below,*
> *Mix with magick to begin my show!*

Erebus plucked a small golden feather from his unfurled wings, held it up to his lips, and blew on it. His breath, mixed with magick, carried the feather slowly, surely, down to the mud and mess below. The instant it touched the earth, there was a *whoosh* that reminded Nyx of how spring rains sounded against a forest canopy, and mist lifted from the mud, carrying the golden feather with it. As sunlight touched the feather, the gold in it expanded, glistened, and changed so that the mud was now covered with mist that held within it all the colors of the rainbow.

"It is not different than what he did before," Kalona muttered.

"Sssh," Nyx whispered to him. "His test isn't completed."

Erebus plucked another feather from his wing. This one was a long, golden pinion. Holding it like a spear, he spoke:

> With borrowed creation, and my own magick, ancient,
> Divine,
> I call to Water, an invocation to join this test of mine.
> Come forth, geyser, rich and radiant in released power
> anew.
> With your might show Nyx that I will ever be faithful
> and true!

Erebus threw the long, golden feather. As if shot from a bow, it sailed in a beautiful arc up and then down, down, to land, sticking its quill into the mud. For a moment nothing happened. Then, just as she was beginning to feel pity for poor Erebus and his failed creation, the earth beneath the feather began to growl and with the sound of waves breaking against a rocky shoreline, the feather was lifted up by a column of water that sprayed high, straight, and strong into the air.

Nyx clapped with pleasure as the geyser continued to spew water and steam through the misty rainbow into the clear blue sky, so high that Nyx would have had no trouble seeing it from the Otherworld. "That's wonderful, Erebus!"

"A powerful and beautiful creation, indeed," Mother Earth agreed.

Erebus landed before Nyx, grinning like a boy. "And

that's not even the best part of it. It will never stop erupting—eternally it will geyser in remembrance of you. Thus I have named it Old Faithful. No matter how long eternity lasts, like this geyser, I will always be your faithful playmate and friend, my Goddess."

"Thank you, Erebus," Nyx said, hugging him. "Your creation has pleased me. You easily passed this test."

Still grinning, Erebus nodded at Kalona. "Your turn, brother."

"Then follow me, and prepare to be impressed!" Before Erebus could protest, Kalona had scooped Nyx into his arms and leaped skyward, rocketing into the west. She peered over his broad shoulder to see Erebus following, with Mother Earth, who was clinging to him, but was also laughing uproariously.

"The Fey are going to have to scurry to catch up with us," she said.

"Yes, and I was hoping so would Erebus, laden with Mother Earth."

"Be kind," she said, but tempered her disapproval by resting her head familiarly on his strong shoulder.

"She dislikes me."

"Be kinder. You always seem so defensive around her."

"Her gaze makes me uncomfortable," he said.

"And still my advice remains the same. Be kind—to Mother Earth, to Erebus, to the mortals that inhabit this realm, and, most important, be kind to yourself."

"You did not mention that I should be kind to you," he said.

Nyx stroked his cheek. "I did not think I needed to." She laid her head against his shoulder again and relaxed into his embrace, hoping silently that the outcome of this test would be very different from the last.

Kalona descended onto a verdant forest filled with the vibrant green of ancient trees. Boulders formed lovely little gorges, and the entire landscape was carpeted with ferns and moss. He came to ground, landing on a group of the largest of the mossy boulders, and gently released her. Before Erebus and Mother Earth had joined them, he kissed her quickly but thoroughly, and said, "Gaze upward." Then he leaped off the boulder, his great wings carrying him aloft so that soon he disappeared into the canopy of green.

Erebus and Mother Earth arrived soon after, and not long after that, a few of the dryads materialized, chattering their displeasure at having been left behind.

"Where is he?" Mother Earth asked.

Nyx pointed upward. "He said to gaze there."

"It is nothing but the side of a hill, littered with steep rocks, moss, and ferns. There aren't even any deer trails leading up there. It is too rocky, too slick," Mother Earth said, gazing upward.

"I wonder what my brother intends," Erebus said.

Nyx smiled at him, noting that he seemed only curious and not envious at all. She linked her arm through his. "You are not mean-spirited at all."

Erebus's smile was sunshine bright. "Why would I waste my time being mean-spirited when being delighted and joyful is so much more fun?"

"An excellent question, young Erebus," Mother Earth said, looking steadily at Nyx. "A wise Goddess would wonder why anyone would choose to be mean-spirited over joyful."

Troubled, Nyx did not meet Mother Earth's gaze. Instead she looked upward, seeking a glimpse of moonlight wings. She was rewarded by his silhouette, dark against the greenery. He was standing on the top ledge of the steep, rocky cliff. Below him, yet still above where Nyx and the rest of them stood, there was a lip of moss-covered rock that formed a basinlike ledge before the boulders opened and dropped down to the forest below.

Kalona raised one arm over his head, hand extended and open, and his voice echoed powerfully against the rocks.

> With her beauty she has captured me,
> Speared through heart and soul I shall always be.
> The mortal realm should rejoice that she is true.
> Forsaking her vow is something Nyx will never do.
> So come to me ancient magick divine.
> Take form in a weapon destined to be mine!

The air above Kalona seemed to shiver, and a long, onyx spear suddenly materialized. Kalona grasped it and commanded:

> *Water, heed the creation gift within my call.*
> *Mirror her most favored headdress in a crystal,*
> > *glistening fall!*

Kalona drove the spear into the boulders at his feet, and water, answering his call, gushed up from within the break in the rock, cascading over the ledge in an ever-increasing powerful spill that widened, sparkling crystal and white, falling into the basin below in perfect mimicry of the glistening headdress of stars that decorated Nyx's hair.

Nyx gasped in pleasure, clapping and laughing. Kalona dropped forward over the ledge to swoop down to her, catching her as she flung herself into his arms.

"Mother Earth! Kalona has re-created your gift that I love so dearly," Nyx said, grinning at her friend when her feet were once more on the ground.

Mother Earth's smile was guarded but genuine. "He has indeed. Well done, Kalona. This does decorate my forest wonderfully, and it will always remind me of the fondness I have for our faithful Goddess."

The dryads trilled in agreement, dancing around the mossy boulders.

Erebus approached Kalona, extending his hand. "It is a thing of beauty, worthy of our Goddess."

Kalona hesitated only a moment. Then he grasped

Erebus's hand. Smiling wryly, he said, "Thank you, brother. And this thing of beauty does not stink."

Erebus threw back his head and laughed. "You win today, brother! And I freely admit it pleases me. You should show your sense of humor more often. I like this Kalona more than the dour, scowling one."

Nyx went to them, and over their clasped hands, she placed her own. "Your brotherhood pleases me more than any test ever could. It is as if Water has filled me to overflowing with joy!"

Joining them, Mother Earth said, "And this is what I intended when I set you to these tests. I wanted only to be sure that worthy companions had been created for our Goddess. I am well pleased today, too. Tell me, Kalona and Erebus, what element will you choose for your final test?"

Nyx nodded to Erebus. "As Kalona chose Water, this next choice is yours."

"If my brother is in agreement, I defer my choice and ask that you decide for me instead."

"I am in agreement with my brother," Kalona said.

Nyx's smile was radiant. "Then I choose Spirit as the element for your final test."

"Very well, then. Until you each call into being your creation, I grant you dominion over Spirit. So I have spoken; so mote it be," said Mother Earth.

"And now I must leave you," Erebus said.

"Leave me?" Nyx smiled questioningly at him.

"Oh, only for now. I do believe the Great Mother and I need to return to Old Faithful," Erebus said, glancing from

Kalona to Nyx, and then sending Mother Earth a pointed look. "We seem to be missing several of the Fey. I think they must still be at the geyser. You know how distracted they can be by sparkling colors."

"We should go collect them, poor dears," Mother Earth readily agreed with him. As Erebus lifted her carefully into his arms, she called, "Come, dryads, let us go back and find your sisters."

Before he leaped skyward, Nyx touched Erebus's arm. "Thank you. You are precious to me."

"As you are to me, my Goddess," he said. "Good-bye, brother. If you need help with your next test you can find me by following the rising sun." The chattering dryads in tow, Erebus took to the sky, leaving Kalona and Nyx completely alone.

"He's smarter than I thought he was, though his height still surprises me," Kalona said.

"His height? The two of you are almost identical."

"He is shorter and younger than me," Kalona said. "Though, as you mentioned the similarity in our appearance, I will admit that he is exceedingly handsome."

"You are incorrigible!" Nyx pushed playfully at his chest.

Laughing, Kalona grabbed her, and fell backward. As Nyx shrieked he unfurled his wings and they floated slowly down to land on a ledge just above the basin that was now filled with crystal water. Still holding her in his arms, Kalona murmured into her ear, "I told you I would never let you fall."

"And have I told you how cold mountain waters are?"

Nyx retorted, looking uncertainly below them at the sparkling pool.

"I cannot command Fire, but you, my Goddess, can," he said.

Nyx grinned. "Yes, I can!" Stepping out of his embrace, she faced the waterfall and lifted her hands, invoking: *I summon you, Fire. Your warmth in these waters I do truly desire.*

Instantly the rocks surrounding the waterfall and pool began to glow like embers, and warm mist lifted from the basin.

"Shall we?" Kalona asked.

"You already know my answer. I am very fond of Water," she said. "I am also very fond of you." Deliberately, the Goddess reached behind her and pulled a silver ribbon, loosening her dress. With a shake of her shoulders, it fell from her body to form a sky-colored puddle at her feet. Wearing only her headdress of stars, she said, "Will you join me?"

"Always," he said, and took her in his arms.

Their attention consumed by the pleasure they found in each other, neither noticed the skeeaed. With eyes narrowed in envy, L'ota watched the immortals' lovemaking before she soundlessly slithered away to disappear into the darkest of shadows.

8.

WHERE THERE IS LIGHT, THERE, TOO, MUST BE DARKNESS...

"Why is this so difficult?" Kalona's frustration boiled over and he threw the rock away from him, causing the ever-watching ravens to flutter and squawk. He had been attempting to breathe Spirit into inanimate objects to create a new type of creature for his Goddess and had thus far failed miserably.

First Kalona had tried to insert consciousness within a tree, one of the gnarled oaks that proliferated the cross-timber area bordering the grassy prairie.

Apparently, trees already contained a living spirit that did not appreciate company. When he had flung spirit into it, the craggy oak had shivered like a horse shaking off a swarm of biting flies, and had hurled Kalona's magick back at him. The immortal had been knocked off his feet with the backlash—and he had had to endure the whoops and chants of the local Shaman who, witnessing the debacle, promptly lit sage and danced all around Kalona's campsite, wafting smoke everywhere. Kalona had no idea what the mortal believed he was doing. He only knew for sure that the smoking sage made his eyes water and his nose tickle, and this annoyed him almost as utterly as did the noisy birds. Rather than smite the human and arouse pesky Mother Earth, Kalona had flown away to Nyx's falls, meaning to wash himself in the crystal shower, hoping cleansing his body would likewise clear his mind.

The Goddess had been there, sunning herself on the moss-covered boulder. As he landed lightly beside her, she'd opened her eyes and smiled joyfully up at him.

"Is it really you, or am I having a wonderful waking dream?"

He'd taken her in his arms and shown her how very real he was.

Kalona had found contentment in Nyx's arms, but that contentment lasted only as long as they were together. When she left him, returning to the Otherworld alone but satisfied, and Kalona had flown back to his campsite, the happiness he'd found in her arms only intensified the frustration he felt at their separation.

"Divine energy, mixed with the power to create and the element Spirit," Thinking aloud, Kalona sat on a felled tree he'd dragged near the campfire he lit nightly, and poked the embers with a long stick. "Spirit, energy, and creation—that equates to life. If I have reasoned through that, Erebus surely will, too. I can see him now, preening and fluttering as he presents his creation to Nyx, making her smile and clap and coo." Kalona jabbed the fire so violently that his stick snapped in half.

"I will not find the answer sitting here staring at the

fire!" That was when Kalona spotted the rock. It was a flat, heart-shaped sandstone. With two hands he hefted it, deciding it would do. With a hasty incantation, Kalona summoned Spirit, mixed it with magick and creation, and funneled it into the lifeless stone.

The rock had broken open, spewing sand and forming grotesque lumps of coagulating energy. Kalona had hurled it away from him in disgust. "Why is it some things can be filled with spirit and life, and others cannot? Humans were once just earth and water. Look at them now!" he'd shouted to the sky.

Some of the grasses surrounding his campsite rustled. Kalona clenched his jaw in irritation. It was probably that damned Shaman again. The human seemed to have devoted the winter years of his life to spying on Kalona.

Three ravens croaked reprovingly at him. Kalona rubbed his aching forehead.

"More in a long list of excellent reasons why I need to complete this test and depart this realm permanently," Kalona grumbled. He had decided days ago that, once he joined Nyx in the Otherworld, he would be able to provide amusements enough for the Goddess *there*, ensuring that she would want to spend less and less time *here*.

As if to lend support to Kalona's plan, the Shaman chose that moment to begin another of his repetitive, unending chants. Kalona sighed and glanced in the direction he'd thrown the misshapen rock. Unsurprisingly, the grasses there were waving, and smudge smoke drifted up, gray against the starry night sky.

"He found the rock." Kalona shook his head. "I should have buried it. Now he'll chant all night, and I will find no peace here."

Kalona spread his wings and prepared to take to the sky. He'd return to Nyx's falls. Perhaps she'd grace him with her presence at dawn, and he could find solace in her arms.

But the immortal hesitated. His instincts told him the answer to the puzzle of the Spirit test was here. This was the prairie Nyx liked so much, peopled by her favorite breed of humans. Surely there was something here that could inspire him to create that which would please Nyx far beyond any colorful show Erebus could concoct.

Kalona began to walk in the opposite direction from where the Shaman's voice lifted and fell in annoying regularity. The night was clear, the moon almost full. Even without his preternatural sight, Kalona would have had no problem finding his way. His father's light shined silver, turning the prairie into a sea of grass. As he walked, Kalona unfurled his wings and lifted his face upward, basking in the soothing light. It calmed him and focused him, so that before long Kalona's frustration had almost completely subsided, replaced by renewed confidence and sense of purpose.

"I will complete this final task and then take my place at her side for eternity. This separation is but a small drop in the sea of time awaiting us," he said.

The grasses a short way behind and to his right rustled.

Sighing, Kalona stopped, turned, and strode purposefully back. "Shaman, this must end. Leave me in peace!" And, conjuring his spear from the magick that drifted in the night sky, Kalona rammed the flat end of it into the ground, creating a clap of thunder.

Not Shaman! L'ota! cried the little Fey as she scurried back from his spear.

"L'ota, do you bring word from Nyx? Does my Goddess summon me?"

Not from Nyx. I watch.

Kalona stifled another sigh. Would nothing go right this night? "Little skeeaed, I'm afraid you're going to be disappointed. There is nothing here to watch except my frustration. Return to the Otherworld. You will fare much better there."

I watch. I help winged one.

"Help me? You mean with the last test?" He chuckled. "Little one, what could you possibly know about Spirit and creation magick?"

The creature's body became more fluid, and her whispery voice took on a cunning lilt. *L'ota know many, many things. L'ota see many, many things.*

"No doubt you do, being so close to Nyx," he said, humoring the creature. "Tell me, L'ota, what should I create for the Goddess?"

Goddess likes jewels—headdress, necklace of crystal, ropes of shells and stones.

Kalona's eyes widened in surprise. "If I could string a

necklace made of living jewels for her, I believe Nyx would be well pleased." He bent and patted the creature. "Thank you, L'ota."

The skeeaed's skin rippled and turned a bright, flushing scarlet. *L'ota know many, many things,* the creature whispered, sounding self-satisfied.

"You do, indeed. Perhaps you can also tell me where I could find some jewels," Kalona said.

Not tell.

"Of course not," he said, looking up to the sky as if to find patience there.

Not tell. Show.

With that, the skeeaed skittered away, motioning with one long arm for Kalona to follow her. *What do I have to lose?* With a shrug of his shoulders, the immortal hurried after the Fey.

L'ota wound her way through the prairie in a serpentine pattern that very quickly convinced Kalona she had no idea where she was leading him.

"L'ota, where exactly are these jewels?"

In cave.

"And where is the cave?"

Follow bull tracks. Find cave.

Kalona had seen the mighty beasts that the Prairie People called bison. They roamed the land in enormous herds. Sometimes there were so many of them they covered the grassland from horizon to horizon. He'd seen a few solitary old bulls, though he had never observed any of the bison, be it bull, cow, or calf, going into a cave.

"L'ota, you are mistaken. Bison do not live in caves."

She paused in her serpentine hunt, looking up at him with a strange light in her almond-shaped eyes. *Not bison. Bull.*

"You are making no sense. I think it is past time that I—"

Tracks of bull! the Fey interrupted him, pointing at the ground where, as she had said, cloven hooves had torn huge indentations into the earth. Kalona was studying the tracks and thinking they had to belong to a beast far larger than any he had seen thus far when L'ota's triumphant shouts of *Cave! Cave!* had him following her again.

The Fey had stopped before the mouth of what appeared to be a rocky split in the earth. It wasn't far from another line of cross-timbers, and it was small enough that it could easily have been overlooked. As Kalona studied it and the enormous tracks that led to it and then disappeared, he realized that it was entirely too small for the bull who made the tracks to have entered.

"L'ota, where did the bull go? He is far too big to fit within the entrance there."

Bull there. The Fey gestured stubbornly to the cave. *I see him. I talk to him.*

Kalona decided the little creature's mind was completely muddled. Perhaps she didn't have the intelligence to truly understand what she was saying. Not that Kalona cared. He only cared that she had the intelligence to lead him to jewels.

"The bull is unimportant. What is important is that there are precious stones within that cave—stones Nyx will find pleasing," he said.

Bull important. White like frost. He not call me servant.

Kalona ran his hand through his hair. Did Nyx know L'ota was mad? If not, how was he to tell her without giving away the fact that he'd used her help to complete the last of the tests?

Above the cave a raven came to ground, croaking at the Fey. The little creature shot it angry looks and seemed ready to bolt.

"Yes, the bull is important," Kalona said, hoping to placate her. "But the jewels are important, too. Are they within?"

Yesssss! L'ota hissed the word.

Deciding that he probably should find a way to tell Nyx that her servant was delusional—*after* he completed the test and joined her in the Otherworld—Kalona dismissed the Fey with a quick smile, saying, "Thank you, little one. The rest of the task I must complete on my own." He had begun to move to the entrance to the cave when the Shaman, as if materializing from the night, appeared before him, holding a turtle rattle in one hand and an eagle-feather-decorated smudge stick in the other.

"Halt, Kalona of the Silver Wings! Do not enter the cave of Darkness. Evil will steal your spirit, and you will wander the earth empty and hopeless, having lost what you value most."

L'ota raised up from the grass that had been concealing her, elongating her body and surprising Kalona by baring sharp, white teeth at the Shaman. *You not a god! You not command him!*

The Shaman whirled to face the Fey, shaking his rattle at her. "Leave this place, demon, friend of an enemy of the People. You do not belong here." He shifted the rattle to the hand that held the smoking stick, reached into a leather pouch that was tied to a shell belt around his waist, and from it flung a handful of blue dust at the skeeaed.

L'ota shrieked and clawed at her face, tearing her flesh. The flesh that she tore writhed, as if it had life of its own. It changed, turning black and serpentine, until finally her entire body exploded, raining the ground with tendrils that continued to slither and writhe and tear at themselves until the Shaman threw another handful of blue dust at the seething nest. There was a terrible shriek that pierced the air, and the tendrils dissolved in a stinking cloud of black smoke.

"You should not traffic with demons, Winged One," the Shaman told him.

Kalona waved a hand in front of his face, trying to dissipate the fetid smoke. "L'ota was one of the Goddess's Fey. What did you do to her, old man?"

"I revealed her true nature, the one she has been hiding with whispers and cunning. She is demon, seduced by Darkness."

"Shaman, none of this makes any sense to me. Have you

nothing better to do than to shadow me and to cause Fey to explode?"

"I caused only the truth to be revealed. And I shadow you because you are the Kalona of the Silver Wings. You have great medicine."

"Yes, I do. And that is why neither talking with a mad Fey, nor going into that cave will cause me harm. No one can steal my spirit."

"Winged One, I have seen you in power dreams given to me by the Great Mother."

"The Great Mother isn't fond of me," Kalona said.

"The Great Mother's wisdom is beyond petty likes and dislikes," retorted the Shaman.

"We may have to agree to disagree about that."

"Kalona of the Silver Wings! You must hear me. In my dreams you are changed. You are filled with anger and despair. You know only violence and hatred. You have lost your way."

"I know my way. It lies there." He pointed at the cave. "And then there." He gestured up, in the direction L'ota had disappeared.

The Shaman's lined face looked sad. His voice lost its strength, and Kalona realized that the man must be very old indeed. "If Darkness follows you from that pit, I am bound by my power dreams and the oath I have sworn to my people to sacrifice to stop it."

"Nothing is following me except you, a mad Fey, and some misguided black birds. Go home, Shaman. Take your woman to your bed. She will help clear your dreams."

The old man began to shuffle his feet in a rhythm that had become familiar to Kalona. "Choose wisely, Winged One. The destiny of many changes with your fate." Chanting in time with his dance, the Shaman finally moved off into the prairie.

Kalona shook his head and waved away more smoke, sending it wafting toward where the birds perched above the cave, making them croak at him in irritation. "At least we are in agreement about this noxious smudging," he muttered at the birds. "The Shaman is a pest." Silently he thought about recent events. How was he going to explain what had happened to L'ota to Nyx? And how would he not get blamed for it?

"Why do I feel Erebus doesn't have these kinds of problems?" Ducking his head, Kalona entered the cave.

The inside of the cave opened so that Kalona could stand easily. There was no light within, and though the immortal could see through darkness, the pit made him shiver. He paused, studying the high, rocky sides, looking for evidence of crystals. Seeing none, Kalona turned his attention to the depths of the cave.

Something glittered just beyond the reach of his vision.

Though he did not like the feeling of confinement the cave gave him, Kalona moved forward. "Just get the Shaman-be-damned jewels and get out." His voice echoed eerily around him, giving him pause.

Into that pause words coursed powerfully through his mind.

Welcome, Kalona, son of the moon, warrior and lover of Nyx. I wondered how long it would take you to come to me.

"Who is there?" Kalona called, reaching up to conjure his spear.

But Kalona's hand remained empty. His spear did not appear.

A rumble of mocking laughter battered through his mind. *You will find there is no magick of the Divine here. Here there is a different kind of power.*

"What are you?" Kalona asked, bracing himself for an attack.

I have been called by many names, and will be called countless more throughout eternity. I am feeling magnanimous today, Kalona. Call me whatever you will. From the depths of the cave, an enormous bull emerged. Its head was so huge that its horns grazed the far-off ceiling, causing a rain of stalactites. The creature's breath was putrid; its coat was the color of a corpse.

Kalona gagged and backed away from it. "Are you the evil of which the Shaman spoke?"

Yes and no. The Shaman's viewpoint is so limiting.

"I will leave you now, but I warn you, if you follow me I will battle you," Kalona said.

Oh, I do hope you and I will battle often, but not today, Kalona. Today I offer you two gifts and ask only one thing in return.

"I want nothing from you."

You do not want your final test to be victorious? You do not want to spend eternity as Nyx's valued warrior, her true and only love?

"What do you know of those things?"

I know all and more. I am more ancient than your Goddess. More ancient than this earth. I have always existed, and I will exist eternally. Where there is Light, there, too, must be Darkness. Without loss there can be no gain. Without pain, how do we know pleasure? Do not pretend you do not understand me. You are not as naïve as your sun-kissed brother. How do you like sharing Nyx with him?

"You go too far, bull!" Kalona turned to leave, but the words that roiled through his mind stopped him.

Cease trying to give Spirit to that which is dead. You do not need to create a new being to please Nyx. You only need to improve one that already exists. That will complete your test and gain you the Otherworld. Though once there, you will spend an eternity sharing your Goddess with another—unless you can offer her more than Erebus.

"I already offer Nyx more than Erebus! I love her beyond what he is capable!"

I approve of your anger, but it will not win the Goddess. Your anger will drive her into your brother's embrace. It already has.

"No. I control my anger."

The bull's laughter battered him again. *You will get better at lying, but you will not get better at controlling your anger. You will have no outlet for it except to hurl it at* golden Erebus, and even at Nyx herself. *That will cause your Goddess to turn her face from you forever.*

"I will not lose her," Kalona said between gritted teeth.

No, you will not if you are valuable to her, and if you have a release for your anger. I can give you both things. I ask only one thing in return, and it is mutually beneficial to us both.

"You may not have my spirit, bull."

I do not want your spirit, Kalona. I simply want entrance to the Otherworld.

The bull's words shocked Kalona silent.

Ah, I see I must explain myself. The Energy that created the Otherworld is as ancient as I, thus it is as powerful as I am, and it is well protected. I can sometimes seep into the shadows of the Otherworld, but never for long. To truly enter there, I must be invited.

"I will never invite that which would destroy my Goddess."

Of course you wouldn't, and I do not ask that of you. I only ask that you invite me to enter occasionally, so that we might do battle. You will win. You will protect your Nyx. She will value you. Your anger will have an outlet, and Erebus will seem a puny playmate in comparison.

"If I win, what do you gain?"

Amusement. I am curious about a realm I cannot fully enter. And, like little L'ota, there are beings in the Otherworld that will welcome my whispers—that would amuse me.

"I will not invite you there. Nyx would never forgive me."

Nyx need never know.

"I will not invite you there. Ever." Kalona said firmly.

You are young. You have no idea how long ever is. Remember this, son of the moon, anger is an invitation of its own. And until you enter it, the Otherworld has known very little anger.

"I will only warn you once, bull. Stay far away from Nyx." Kalona backed toward the mouth of the cave.

It is you who will bring me close to your Goddess. As surely as Mother Earth created humans, your jealousy will create anger. That anger, arrogant godling, will allow me entrance to Nyx's realm!

With the white bull's mocking laughter ringing throughout his mind, Kalona fled the cave.

From the cover of the tall grasses, the Shaman watched Kalona of the silver wings flee the pit, and saw the Darkness that slithered from the maw of the evil place. Snakelike and silent, tendrils followed the immortal. The immortal did nothing to stop them.

The Shaman bowed his head in sad resignation. Often he wished his dreams were less accurate, that he was like the rest of the People, naïve about the life journey unfolding before them. This particular moment, he almost cursed his gift. The Great Mother had shown him what he must do if the Winged One began trafficking with Darkness, and though it would break his heart and perhaps even incur the wrath of a Goddess, he would not falter.

Shoulders stooped, the old man headed back to his lodge to make ready for what must come. The next night would be that of a full moon—the hunting full moon. He would make the sacrifice then, and pray to the Great Mother that what he offered would appease Darkness enough to keep the terrible future he had glimpsed from coming to the People.

9.

MUCH LATER, DURING THE EONS SHE HAD TO REPLAY
IN HER MIND THE EVENTS THAT LED TO HEARTBREAK
AND TRAGEDY, NYX OFTEN BLAMED HERSELF...

The encounter with the white bull shook Kalona to his core. The creature had been loathsome, and what he had proposed was impossible, but the bull's words held a despicable truth that the winged immortal could not deny. That truth began to circle round and round Kalona's mind, an endless reminder of his own fear—his own vulnerability.

He could not share Nyx with Erebus. He would not be able to control his anger if Erebus became Nyx's lover because he would not be able to bear the despair her infidelity would cause him.

Miserable, Kalona flew to Nyx's falls, hoping to find his Goddess there. The falls were empty of all but the shadow of her beauty.

He went to the blue lake and sat beside the boat he had carved her, waiting for her to appear. Nyx did not appear.

Kalona even searched for the mad little Fey, L'ota, but even though he thought he caught glimpses of her hiding within the shadows, she refused to answer his call.

He hated not being able to summon his Goddess. He

didn't want to control her; that wasn't it at all. He simply needed a way to speak with her, to touch her, to be in her presence. Only Nyx could soothe the despair building within him. Only Nyx could reassure him and heal that which the bull's knowing words had broken.

Kalona was utterly hopeless without Nyx, and from his hopelessness grew frustration.

Where was she? Why was she leaving him alone? Did she no longer love him? Did she no longer desire him? Did she not need him as he needed her?

Was Nyx with Erebus instead of him?

In despair, unable to concentrate on completing the final test he must pass before he would be allowed entrance to Nyx's realm, Kalona took to the sky, searching the world not for Nyx, but for his brother, the golden son of the sun.

"There! Is it finally ready? Have I forgotten anything?" Nyx ran her hand over the fur-covered pallet and looked around the spacious chamber she had chosen for Kalona.

Have forgotten the golden one.

"Erebus? Don't be silly, L'ota. I prepared his chamber earlier. It is there, on the side of the palace that opens to the morning sunlight."

Not beside your chamber.

"No, there is only one room that adjoins my chamber and—" The Goddess broke off her explanation with a shake of her head. "L'ota, is something amiss with you? You seem not yourself recently. Are you spending too much time on earth? I hope I haven't over-tired you by asking you to check on Kalona for me and to help ready these chambers." The Goddess paused to smile at the skeeaed. "It is just that I depend upon you, even more than I do your sisters. You have long taken very good care of me, L'ota. Would you like to join the dryads as they frolic in the mortal realm below? They must enjoy it. They never seem to tire."

I do not frolic. L'ota fidgeted while she whispered her answer to Nyx. The Goddess thought she looked uncharacteristically nervous.

"Well, it is true that skeeaeds are more serious than dryads, but you might find that a little frolicking is fun."

Do you command it so?

"Of course not! I don't command you, or any of the Fey, to frolic. I simply meant that you do look tired and that I am sorry if I have wearied you. L'ota, tonight I want you to rest. Do not be concerned about Kalona, Erebus, or me. Tonight, little one, is just for you." The Goddess smiled at the Fey and patted the soft tuft of her hair.

L'ota bowed her head and said, *You command. I obey.* Then she slid into the shadows and disappeared from the chamber, leaving the Goddess shaking her head and sighing. "Though they have been with me for eons, the Fey remain such strange creatures. Sometimes I believe they understand too much; sometimes I believe it is too little. Well, a rest from her duties should replenish her energy, whether she asked for it or not." Nyx looked around the chamber again and smiled. "And I have been keeping her very busy readying the palace for the presence of Kalona and Erebus."

"Kalona . . ." Nyx repeated his name, loving the sound of it. Oh, how she had missed him! She had purposefully kept herself from visiting him so that he would not be distracted and would be well and quickly prepared for the final test. And Kalona was obviously in agreement with her; he had not once called for her, though L'ota had visited him daily and waited patiently to bring his summons back to Nyx. Thus, Nyx believed his greatest desire was the same as hers—to complete the final test as quickly as possible so that he could join her in the Otherworld for an eternity!

Now the palace was ready, though so very empty. And Kalona was so very close! Perhaps she could visit him once, for only a part of the evening. She would show him how eager she was to have him by her side, and then leave him to his preparations.

The winged one calls for you. As if Kalona had read her mind, L'ota was suddenly there, whispering the words the Goddess had secretly longed for days to hear. *He is at the geyser.* L'ota wrinkled her nose in remembrance of the smell of the place.

Nyx laughed gaily. "How kind of him to choose to meet me at Old Faithful! It shows that he has truly rid himself of his jealousy of Erebus. Oh, L'ota! Could he be more perfect?" The Goddess hugged the Fey, picking up the little creature and dancing playfully around the beautifully decorated chamber that awaited her lover.

Nyx was still laughing when she let go of the skeeaed and hurried to choose something lovely and sheer to wear, too distracted to hear the last hissing words the creature would speak to her: *Yesssss, L'ota watch. L'ota tell. L'ota show you!*

Much later, during the eons she had to replay in her mind the events that led to heartbreak and tragedy, Nyx often blamed herself. Had she not been so girlish, so giddy, so ungoddesslike, she might have stopped to question the whys and hows of things and prevented the horror of what was to come. But she hadn't. Nyx hadn't once truly wondered why L'ota had become so distant and defensive. She hadn't questioned why she didn't feel Kalona's presence as she materialized at the geyser. She hadn't been wise enough even to consider whether the Darkness she had been sensing, though unable to reach her, had the power to influence others.

No, Nyx had lacked in wisdom and experience, and because of that lack, she and many others paid a price too dear for simple forgiveness.

That evening Nyx knew nothing of future pain and regret. That evening all she knew was that she intended to spend it in the arms of her beloved.

Which was why the Goddess was completely taken aback when she materialized on the ridge overlooking the geyser and was greeted by Erebus's exclamation of "My Goddess! What a lovely surprise it is to see you! I admit that I had been thinking of you and wishing for your opinion on my discovery. So, you appearing here is, indeed, fortuitous."

"Merry meet, Erebus." Nyx quickly recovered her composure. Had L'ota actually said which winged one had called for her? "What is this discovery of yours?"

"Come with me." Smiling, he held his hand out to her. "I found them in a den made within the roots of an old tree, just there." He pointed into the tree line above them, helping Nyx to climb over the rocky outcroppings. "Careful," he said, lifting her over a cluster of brambles.

He led Nyx to a fragrant cedar tree. Pressing his finger against his lips, he carefully pulled back the frond of a fern to reveal a neat little den nestled within the tree's massive roots. Within the den were five plump, furry creatures.

"Kittens!" Nyx exclaimed, causing the babies to wake and blink at her with bright, curious eyes.

"So, she was right. The wildcats do please you," Erebus said, sounding satisfied with himself. "They aren't frightened of you, though they do not thus favor anyone else." At the sound of his voice, the kittens had bowed their backs and made hissing, spitting noises at him.

Nyx laughed and stroked them, calming their miniature fury. "Of course they are not frightened of me. They recognize their Goddess. And they do please me, very much! So much so that I have actually secreted one away to the Otherworld with me." Nyx glanced at Erebus. *"She?"*

Erebus's grin made him look boyishly adorable. "Mother Earth, of course."

"Of course. There's little that can be kept secret from the Great Mother."

"Does that bother you?"

"No, not at all. I cherish her friendship and the affection she has for me. Does it bother you?"

"No! I love the Great Mother and the mortal realm. There are such interesting creatures that populate it. And, I owe her a vast debt—that of my creation."

"You are truly kind and generous, Erebus."

"Thank you, my Goddess. Would you sit with me awhile and wait for your geyser to erupt so that we might watch it together?"

"I would love to," Nyx assured him. Before he closed the den with the frond, she gave the kittens one last, lingering look. "Did Mother Earth happen to mention to you if she would mind if I *secreted* away a few more wildcats?"

Erebus laughed. "No, she did not, though I will ask it of her when next she and I visit."

"So you visit her regularly?" Nyx asked as they made their way back to the ridge overlooking the geyser.

"Yes. I enjoy her company, though I do not understand her obsession with the Fey."

"I would warn you to get used to them, but they seem to prefer the mortal realm to that of the Otherworld. Even my skeeaed has been temperamental lately."

"Skeeaed. Is that the little pink-colored Fey who is so often in your shadow?"

"Yes, L'ota. Did you not speak with her today?"

"No, I haven't seen the creature since the last test," Erebus said. Then he stopped and lifted her off her feet. "Goddess, there are brambles everywhere and the rocks are sharply edged. The next time you visit me here, I would ask that you remember to wear shoes."

"I'll do that," she said. "But until then I will appreciate your gallantry."

When they reached the ridge, Erebus put her gently down on a smooth-sided boulder that made a perfect chair. He sat on the rocky ground beside her, and they faced the geyser. Neither of them spoke, but the silence between them was not uncomfortable. Nyx was thinking how pleasant and peaceful it was there, and how the rank smell hardly reached the ridge, when the earth began to growl and then whooshing waves announced the coming water and the column erupted into the air going up, up against the crimson-and-pink sunset.

Nyx took Erebus's hand. "It is so pretty! Thank you again for creating a thing of such beauty for me."

"Your smile is thanks enough," Erebus said. Then he tilted his head and his golden gaze caught hers, searching. "You should go to him."

Nyx blinked in surprise. "Him?"

"Kalona. You should go to him. He needs you. With you, he is a better being than he is without you."

"I was giving him time to—" Nyx stopped herself, not wanting to appear uncaring of Erebus's feelings.

"You were giving him time to focus on the final test without the distraction of your loveliness," Erebus finished for her. "I am sure that that seemed a good idea, but if I know my brother, and I have come to realize that I do know him, as he is really just another version of myself, I can tell you that solitude does not bring him focus. He needs you," Erebus repeated.

"Do you never feel jealous of what he and I share?"

"No, my bright, beautiful Goddess. I am content with that destiny for which I was created. I would not make a very good warrior."

"I wasn't speaking of the warrior part," she said softly, meeting his sunlit eyes.

His smile was warm. "If you ever desire me to be your lover, I would most willingly and happily return that desire—as frequently or as infrequently as you might want me. But I have no wish to claim your body as mine and mine alone. My only wish is for your happiness, and I believe my brother at your side, being your warrior *and* your lover is what would make you happiest. It would also make him happiest, which is important to me, though I am sure it will take me eons to convince Kalona of that."

Nyx slid from her rock stool onto Erebus's lap, where she threw her arms around him and hugged him tightly. "You do make me happy, so very happy!"

"Then I shall not interrupt that happiness."

From Erebus's embrace, Nyx looked up at the darkening sky to see Kalona hovering above them, his voice as flat and emotionless as his expression.

"Brother! Come, join us," Erebus said, standing and carefully helping Nyx back to her rocky seat. "We were just speaking of you."

"I heard only your Goddess's voice," Kalona said, not looking at Nyx. "And she spoke of the great happiness you bring her. Nyx, with your permission, I will leave you to that."

"You have my permission," Nyx said, her voice sounding very young.

With a flash of silver wings, Kalona disappeared into the horizon.

Erebus sighed. "For a warrior he seems awfully sensitive."

"He loathes me," Nyx said.

"He loves you," Erebus corrected. "That is why he has flown away in a jealous fit. All you need do is find him and explain *why* you said that I make you very happy. Later I will mention to him that if he is going to eavesdrop, he should learn to do a more thorough job of it."

"Erebus, you are a good friend," Nyx said, bending to kiss his cheek.

"And you are a kind and loving Goddess," Erebus said. "Oh, and I am ready to complete the final test."

"Shall we summon Spirit to call Mother Earth?"

"There is time aplenty for that. I can wait a little while until you have made peace with my brother."

Nyx hugged him again and then she stood and, thinking of Kalona, called the magick of Divinity to her. It lifted her and, leaving a trail of glittering starlight in her wake, began to carry the Goddess toward the sea of grass that covered the center of the wild continent.

10

FOR MY DAUGHTER, THIS CREATION OF MINE,
I GIVE THE GIFT OF NIGHT DIVINE...

Nyx found his campsite easily, though Kalona was absent from it. She meant to leave quickly, to follow the connection she had with him and go directly to him, but the spot Kalona had made his own intrigued her.

It was at the edge of the grassy prairie where it curved into the cross-timber section of trees that lined a sandy creek, at the other end of which the Prairie People had a large settlement. Nyx thought it was a nice spot for a camp, and Kalona had certainly made it comfortable.

She looked through the piles of pelts, woven baskets, tools, and foodstuff, realizing that her lover had obviously made friends with the Prairie People—or she hoped he had. Nyx's hand lingered on a particularly thick fur, much like the one he had lined her boat with the day he had crafted it for her.

What was Kalona trading for such a rich array of gifts? Nyx knew the native mortals—knew them well. They could be kind and generous, but they also rarely gave without purpose.

A small sliver of apprehension lodged with the Goddess

as she remembered Kalona's first encounter with the Prairie People. They had named him a winged God and had been ready to worship him.

"No! I will not think ill of Kalona. He is not responsible for the superstitions of the Prairie People," Nyx told herself firmly.

The Goddess turned her face from the pile of gifts and left the cozy little campsite. She stood at the edge of the prairie and spread her arms wide, throwing back her head and drinking in the rising light of a full, silver moon. The night was clear, and the sky was filled with stars. The breeze was warm and gentle, and out into it Nyx sent her magick.

"Lead me to my love, so that I might make right what has become wrong between us," Nyx commanded the night.

Wisps of magick, like the sparkling tail of shooting stars, flowed from the Goddess. Gently but surely they pulled her forward. Nyx followed. Confident that Kalona was nearby, she felt her heartbeat quicken in anticipation. He had been created for her; he did love her. She need only to look into his amber eyes, to touch the smooth strength of his body, and he would know as surely as she that there was nothing and nobody standing between them, that there never would be.

Nyx saw the black birds before she saw Kalona. They pulled her gaze to a distant rolling rise in the prairie that held a few small trees and some lichen-covered sandstone ledges. She could see Kalona's silhouette. He was sitting on a large, flat slab of stone, head in his hands, shoulders bent. His wings glistened as if they were absorbing the light of the full moon. Nyx stopped and stood silently, watching him from a distance. *He is so beautiful, so majestic, and so sad,* she thought. *I ache to ease his sadness.*

Nyx had just begun to close the distance between herself and Kalona when a figure moved in the upper corner of the Goddess's vision, drawing her gaze from the winged immortal. Above him, on an even larger outcropping of sandstone rock, a feather-bedecked old man had appeared. He stood, slowly straightening his age-crooked body. As he straightened, Nyx could see that he was not alone. A woman was with him—a girl, really. She was wearing an elaborately decorated dress of tanned hide, which Nyx thought was quite lovely. Actually, even from a distance the Goddess could tell that the maiden was spectacularly beautiful.

Nyx's brow raised and she felt a stab of jealousy. Was the old man offering the maid to Kalona? What if he accepted her?

The Goddess was torn. Part of her wanted to fade into the night and to allow her love to take his pleasure where he could find it.

Another part of her wanted to rush forward and demand Kalona choose none other but her.

Nyx bowed her head and surrendered the knowing of what it felt to be jealous and vulnerable and full of despair.

The old man began to chant a wordless, rhythmic melody.

His voice was hypnotic, and Nyx felt her own bare feet begin to move in time with it when Kalona spoke.

"Shaman, enough! I have endured too many miseries today. I do not need your unending song added to them." He raised his head, and Nyx could see his body jerk in surprise. "Why have you brought a child here?"

"I do only as my dream commands."

"About that dream, you could have told me that—"

The old man's voice cut across Kalona's. As he sang his song, the timbre of his voice changed, magnified with a strange power that glowed from the center of his forehead in a pure, white light the shape of a crescent moon.

> *What I do, I do for two*
> *One for her*
> *And one for you*
> *Take this maid*
> *Her blood runs true*
> *Sacrifice for two*
> *One for her*
> *And one for you*

Mesmerized, Nyx watched and listened, but as the Shaman's song progressed, a terrible sense of foreboding filled the Goddess and she began to move forward, slowly at first, and then more quickly, until she was running.

> *Balance hold*
> *New and old*

Scale of two
One for her
And one for you!

With the last line of his song, the Shaman lifted his hand. Nyx saw that in it he held a long, sharp obsidian blade.

"No!" the Goddess cried.

The Shaman's blade did not waver. It slashed the maid's throat, releasing a torrent of blood. She fell to his feet, gasping her life's breath and flooding the sandstone with a crimson tide.

"Why have you done this?" Nyx rushed to the maid, pulling the dying girl into her arms.

"The sacrifice was for two. One for him. One for you. Forgive me, Goddess. I did only what I could do." Then the old man's eyes rolled white. He clutched his chest and fell into the grasses, breathing no more.

Nyx looked up to see that Kalona's face was as pale as moonlight. "What madness is this?"

"I-I do not know. I thought the old man deluded, misguided even. I did not think him capable of this."

"Have he and his People been worshipping you?"

Nyx saw genuine surprise in Kalona's expression. "They left me gifts, and the old man often chanted and smudged around me. Is that worship?" Kalona shook his head, staring at the dying maiden. "I am a fool. I am to blame for these two deaths."

"No!" Nyx said sternly, not willing to allow Kalona to fall into despair and guilt. "He was an old man. His heart failed him. That could not be changed and is not your fault. But this girl, this child, he so mistakenly sacrificed to you, she still clings to life. We can save her, you and I. Give me your borrowed gift of creation, and invoke Spirit. What would please me most is that your final test save the life of this girl."

"But Mother Earth—"

"I am Goddess! And I proclaim that I am willing to exchange my friendship with Earth for this child's life."

Kalona bowed his head to her. "Yes, my Goddess."

> *I call you, Spirit, Power Divine, and creation magick as*
> *well.*
> *I have one more test to pass, one more tale to tell.*
> *As the Goddess commands, so mote it be,*
> *However she wishes to use you, with her I agree.*

Kalona bent and kissed Nyx gently on the lips, and as the Goddess accepted his kiss, she drew within her body Spirit, the magick of creation, and the power of the Divine.

Nyx lifted the obsidian knife from where the old man had dropped it, quickly slashing the blade across her own wrist. Then she held the oozing line to the girl's pale lips, saying:

> *Blood of my blood, you shall ever after be.*
> *Take, drink. From this night forth your new life is*
> *my decree.*

The girl's eyes remained closed, but her lips opened against the Goddess's wound, and she drank as Nyx commanded.

The Goddess bent and blew gently on the girl's bleeding throat. The torn flesh instantly began to mend.

> *For my daughter, this creation of mine,*
> *I give the gift of Night Divine.*

Nyx kissed the girl's lips, breathing the last of Spirit within her, and then she kissed the middle of the girl's smooth forehead, touching the child with a Goddess's Old Magick, whispering, *With this Mark tattoo, your life begins anew.*

In the middle of the girl's forehead a sapphire-colored crescent moon appeared. From it, spreading down either side of the girl's face, grew an intricate series of filigreed swirls and mysterious signs that held symbols of each of the five elements, magickally mirroring the tattoos with which Nyx so often chose to decorate her own body.

The girl opened her eyes. "Great Goddess of Night, tell me your name so that I may worship you."

"You may call me Nyx."

Then the night around them exploded as Mother Earth materialized, followed by a crowd of trilling dryads who took one look at their Goddess and fell unusually silent.

"Ah, so, it is as I thought," Mother Earth said. She shook her head sadly. "The test has been tainted. Kalona must fail."

Erebus dropped from the sky, holding a woven basket. His sunlit smile faded as he took in the somber scene.

"I felt the test begin. I hurried to join you," Erebus said.

"Daughter, sleep, and when you awaken you will forget the terror of your creation and remember only love, always love," Nyx commanded the maiden, and brushed a hand down her face, causing the girl's eyes to close. Then the Goddess moved her gently off her lap, and stood to face Erebus and Mother Earth.

"What happened here is my responsibility. The old man was confused and mistaken. He sacrificed this maiden to Kalona in a fit of madness. I commanded Kalona give me his creation gift and invoke Spirit, so that I might mix our magick and save her life. His actions have pleased me. I decree that Kalona has passed the third and final of his tests." Nyx turned to Erebus. "You may complete your test now, as well."

With none of the playfulness he usually exhibited, Erebus walked to Nyx and placed the basket on the ground between her and the sleeping maiden.

"I meant this as a gift for the Prairie People you love so well," he told her. "It seems right that they now belong to your most favored mortal daughter."

Erebus took the lid from the basket to reveal the five kittens Erebus had shown her earlier that evening. He spread his hands over the basket, and invoked:

Ancient Magick, borrowed creation, and the power
of Spirit I call to thee.

Know my will and do as I command from the very
  heart of me.
Create joy from this night of confusion, death, and
  tears.
Comfort this daughter of Nyx with companionship
  during long years.
Familiars and friends and playmates they shall be in
  name and in heart.
Once chosen, by the might of the sun they will never
  be apart.

Erebus's hands blazed with the orange glow of a setting sun, and when he lifted them from the top of the basket, Nyx saw that the wild tan and gray fur of the kittens had been changed to sunlight orange and cloudy cream. Erebus lifted one of the kittens from the basket, and instead of hissing and scratching, it began to purr, nuzzling him with its fluffy face. The winged immortal smiled. "Not me, sweet one. She has need of your friendship more than I." He tucked the kitten beside the sleeping maiden, and then carried the other four to the girl, as well, so that they formed a warm circle against her. Then he turned back to Nyx.

The Goddess took his face in her hands and kissed him gently. "Your gift has pleased me greatly. You, too, have passed the last of the tests." Then Nyx turned to face Mother Earth. "I did not plan what happened tonight."

"And I planned too rigidly. I tried to control too much. Tonight I realize that there are some things that not even your great capacity to love or my gift for creation can forestall."

"Are we still friends?"

"Always," Mother Earth said. "But I think it is time I stopped meddling in your personal affairs."

"I will never be able to thank you enough for that loving meddling. You ended my loneliness and now, with Kalona and Erebus, the Otherworld will be filled with life again."

"You are more than welcome," Mother Earth said. She walked to Erebus and embraced him warmly. "You will always be the memory of a perfect, sun-filled summer's day to me. I have enjoyed being your mother."

"And I enjoy being your son. Will we not continue our visits?"

"Perhaps, but I think you will find that you will be quite busy in the Otherworld, and I realize that I have become weary again. I need to sleep." Mother Earth accepted Erebus's kiss on her cheek, then she moved to stand before Kalona. "I have been hard on you, my moonlit son, but that is because of what I sense within you. Kalona, you are a different type of creation from your brother. You were born warrior and lover, and those two roles are not easy to bear side by side. I see within you a limitless capacity for good, as well as an equally limitless capacity for harm. Through the tests I meant for you to learn that with great power comes great responsibility. Only your future choices will show whether I succeeded in my lessons."

"I do not intend harm," Kalona said earnestly.

"Intent is a fickle friend," Mother Earth said. "You did not intend for any mortals to die this night, did you?"

"No. I did not."

"And yet one is dead, and one is altered forever. Kalona, *hear me well as this I vow: Should your anger, Darkness allow, Earth's embrace shall not succor thee. So I have spoken, so mote it be.*" Sealing the oath, Mother Earth kissed him on his cold lips and then turned to Nyx wearily. The two women embraced.

Nyx's gaze went to the maiden. "When you are not sleeping, would you watch over my daughter with me? She is a new being, and the only one of her kind. She will need special care, and one cannot have too many mothers."

"My friend, I am afraid that I may sleep so long that in some ways I shall never again arise, so before I drift into my living bed, I will create once more, though you must watch over these children yourself."

Nyx was confused for a moment, and then she understood what Mother Earth intended. "You will create more like her!"

"I will, though their creation will be more difficult than was hers. She is not truly a *new* being, but rather a mortal made *more*. I will sow humanity with the seeds of what she is. I do not know how many of them will be able to become *more*."

Nyx clasped her friend's hands. "Thank you, Mother Earth. Thank you for making sure my daughter will not live her life alone."

"Do not thank me yet. I do not know how many like her will survive."

"Humans are strong and brave. There will be many who survive," Nyx said. "And I will be their Goddess of Night!"

"Yes, my friend. Yes," Mother Earth agreed. "Now, embrace me again, and take your leave quickly. I want no sadness or regret between us."

Nyx hugged her tightly. "Sleep in peace with no worry and no regret. I will visit your children, and I will watch over that which is eternal within them for eternity."

"Watch over yourself as well," Mother Earth said. Then, still embracing the Goddess, she whispered for her ears alone: "And watch Kalona. If he begins to change it will be because his anger has grown greater than his love. If he allows anger to consume him, it will also consume you and your realm." Then she released Nyx and stepped back. "Go now, and may you all be blessed—"

Heartbreaking trills erupted from the group of Fey that clustered around Mother Earth. Nyx saw that there weren't only dryads there, but coblyn, naiads, and even a few skee-aeds had appeared on the prairies, painting the night with bright colors that reflected their anxiety.

"No, little ones, do not despair. You belong in the Otherworld—that is your home," Mother Earth said.

"Oh, my friend, please tell me that the Fey may continue to visit your earth," Nyx said.

Mother Earth looked surprise. "You would allow it?"

Nyx smiled warmly at the Fey. *As long as there is Old*

Magick, ancient, rich and true, there you shall find the Fey, and there they shall find you.

"So your Goddess has spoke, and so mote it be!" Mother Earth cried, enlivened again as the Fey formed a circle around her and began to dance in celebration.

Nyx wiped away a tear, and then took Kalona and Erebus by the hand. "Let us leave her now, happy and surrounded by those who bring her such joy," she said softly, guiding them into the darkness of the grassy prairie. When they were out of sight of Mother Earth, Nyx let loose their hands and said, "Follow me." The Goddess lifted her hand and a slender silver thread appeared, as if the moon had lent her a beam of light. She grasped it and smiled at the winged immortals who were studying her with twin looks of apprehension. "Don't worry. If you know the way, the journey is not far. And I will show you the way, so that ever after you will never be far from me." Then the glittering ribbon went taut, lifting the Goddess into the night sky. Kalona and Erebus unfurled their wings together, and took to the sky after her.

Nyx didn't let loose the glittering silver thread until, out of the complete blackness that exists between realms, a patch of hard-packed earth suddenly appeared. She stepped on it and turned to face Kalona and Erebus.

"Is it a piece of Mother Earth here?" Erebus asked, bending to touch the ground that looked so very much like the red dirt from the tall grass prairie.

"There's more of it in there," Kalona said, pointing at a seemingly endless grove that stretched before them.

"No, there is nothing of Mother Earth here," Nyx said. "Though you will see many sights that will remind you of her."

Nyx thought Kalona looked relieved. Erebus only looked curious. "What is that tree?" he asked, starting to walk forward toward it.

Nyx stepped before him, blocking his way. Both immortals were now looking at her curiously.

"That tree has many names in the mortal realm, Yggdrasil, Abellio, and the Hanging Tree are but three of many reflections of its Old Magick. Here, I call it the Wishing Tree, as I have filled it with ribbons of Divine Energy in which I have woven wishes and dreams, joy and love. It stands at the entrance to my realm, the Otherworld. I intend to share my realm with both of you, but before I allow you entrance I ask each of you to make me one promise—that no matter what the eternity to come brings, you will never again speak of the events of this night. My daughter, and those who come after her, must never know that they were mistakes created because of superstition and madness. Do you agree?"

"I do, and you have my promise," Kalona said.

"As do I. You have my promise as well, kind, loving Goddess," Erebus said.

"Then I gladly bid you enter the Otherworld, and wish that together we will all blessed be!"

Mother Earth left the Fey to their endless dancing. She had one last task to perform before she could sleep, but first she approached the body of the Shaman. She knelt beside him and closed his sightless eyes; then she waved her hands over his body, and the rich earth of the prairie parted, gently making an opening in which to cradle the old man.

"You did well, just as I asked. I know it broke your heart to follow my edict and sacrifice the maiden, but by doing so you have given Kalona his only chance at redemption, for he has, indeed, been tainted by Darkness. Nyx does not see it, but I see it as clearly as did you. You did as I commanded. Now I will keep my word to you, old one." Mother Earth touched his forehead, and drew from within him the glowing orb that held his eternal spirit.

Come to me, mighty beast of the grass sea!

An enormous bison trotted up to Mother Earth. The muscles of his wide chest rippled as he bowed before her, his muzzle resting by her knee. She stroked his thick pelt, murmuring her appreciation of his majesty. Then she completed her promise by saying:

Joined for a lifetime you and he shall be!

She pressed the spirit glob against the bison's forehead, and it disappeared within the beast. Mother Earth smiled up at him. "Go, old one made young! Roam the prairie and have a long, fertile life."

With a snort, the bison obeyed her, and as he trotted away he kicked the air in a joyous dance of freedom.

THOUGH IT WOULD CREATE A WOUND WITHIN HER THAT WOULD ACHE FOR ETERNITY, NYX KNEW KALONA MUST BE STOPPED...

And so the eons passed. At first, all was well in the Otherworld. The Goddess was no longer alone. She had warrior and lover, playmate and friend. Nyx thrived, and thus did the Otherworld.

Nyx's children, created by Mother Earth before she retreated to sleep within herself, thrived as well, though both immortals had been right. Many were not strong enough to survive the Change, but those who did were the best of humanity—the bravest and strongest, the brightest and most talented. In solidarity, they named themselves vampyre, the children of Nyx, and they evolved a society that honored women as Goddess, and valued men for their roles of warrior and lover, playmate and friend. Nyx was so well pleased by her children that she sometimes passed along gifts to them based on the five elements over which her friend had granted her dominion. But no matter how much they pleased her, or how many times Nyx granted the vampyres gifts, the Goddess made quite certain that she did not meddle too often in their lives. Mother Earth had taught her a valuable lesson. Love cannot thrive if it is too closely controlled. Nyx vowed that she would not control her beloved children, that they would always have free will, whether they chose to use that freedom wisely or not.

Though she was sometimes sorry she had made that vow, the Goddess never broke her oath.

Nyx was also sometimes sorry that she had vowed never to speak of the night the first of her children had been created. The vow had been well intended—made to protect her children. What the Goddess had not realized then was that by cloaking that night in silence, she had also lost the opportunity to explain many things to Kalona, and in return to ask him for an explanation for many things as well.

They never spoke of what had happened when Kalona had appeared at the geyser, or of the strange superstition that had caused the Shaman to make blood sacrifice to Kalona.

In her mind Nyx often replayed the chant the Shaman had sung before he sacrificed the girl.

What I do, I do for two
One for her
And one for you . . .

What had the old man meant? Nyx believed the "you" of which he had chanted was Kalona. Could the "her" not have meant the maiden, but instead have been referring to the Goddess herself?

The not knowing haunted Nyx, especially as, bound by her own vow, she could speak her questions to no one, especially not Kalona, who seemed increasingly not to want to speak to her about many things.

Nyx tried to talk with Kalona about Mother Earth, whom she missed terribly. Kalona avoided the subject of his symbolic mother and grew silent.

When Nyx wondered aloud what could have happened to little L'ota, who disappeared the same night Erebus and Kalona entered the Otherworld, Kalona had only silence as reply.

Kalona's silence began to lengthen and spread, until there was little he and Nyx were able to speak about, and the only thing that was not awkward between them was the flame that burned when their bodies joined.

But Nyx needed more than wordless passion to be happy, and she found herself more and more often turning to Erebus for companionship. The golden immortal was not her lover, but he served the role of Consort more fully than did Kalona. Erebus spoke with her easily; there was nothing hidden between them. Erebus truly listened to her, without pride or jealousy, and Erebus had the ability to make her laugh.

The more Nyx turned to Erebus, the more withdrawn Kalona became, until he stopped seeking even the solace of joining his body with the Goddess. In the malignant silence that grew between them, Kalona was filled with a jealousy that had never truly been reconciled, and the anger created by that jealousy.

It was then that Darkness began its attack on the Otherworld.

The first time it happened, Nyx had been sunning herself on Erebus's balcony, taking in the morning light. She remembered that Erebus had made a feather toy for the wildcat that followed Nyx throughout the Otherworld, and that she had been laughing like a girl at the cat's obsession with the feather when something dark and terrible had slithered over the edge of the balcony and wrapped itself around the cat's hind leg, causing it to yowl in pain.

Nyx had screamed in fear, and Kalona had suddenly appeared like an avenging God, wings spread, eyes glowing amber. He had skewered the slithering creature with his obsidian spear. Nyx had scooped up the cat and run into Kalona's arms. He had held her, stoking her hair and whispering reassurances to her, until she had stopped trembling.

"What was that?" Nyx had asked him.

"Darkness," Kalona had said in a voice filled with anger.

"How did it gain entrance here?" Erebus had asked as he gently bandaged the cat's bleeding leg.

"You tell me, brother. It was you who was alone with the Goddess when it struck."

Erebus had had no answer for his brother, and neither had Nyx. But what had begun that day continued to spread until almost every day Kalona battled some kind of Darkness.

In the beginning the attacks brought Kalona and Nyx together once more. They became lovers again for a brief, beautiful time. The Goddess sought his company, and they found a way to speak to each other. Kalona even happily agreed to visit the mortal realm with Nyx while she made an appearance to her favored children, the vampyres, as they christened the first House of Night after their Goddess of Night.

But that visit ended in jealousy and anger when Nyx remarked joyfully, "Look, Kalona, there are so many cats here! They are such loving familiars of my children."

"Yes, I am sure Erebus will be thrilled at the joy his gift still brings you," Kalona had quipped, and then fallen silent.

Nyx could say nothing—not about the gift he had given her that night, and how that gift pleased her more than any mortal creature could. No, Nyx could say nothing. Her own vow silenced her. She could only watch as jealousy and anger warred within Kalona.

As they returned to the Otherworld, a great horned creature of many heads and with teeth like daggers, had attacked them. Kalona destroyed it, escorted Nyx to her chambers and then, without speaking, he left her there, alone, while he searched for more enemies to slay.

That night Nyx wept bitterly as Mother Earth's warning echoed from her memory: . . . *watch Kalona. If he begins to change, it will be because his anger has grown greater than his love. If he allows anger to consume him, it will also consume you and your realm.*

Nyx realized it was happening. Kalona's anger was consuming their love and the Otherworld, as well. Though it would create a wound within her that would ache for eternity, Nyx knew Kalona must be stopped.

"You summoned me?"

Nyx had dressed carefully, choosing the gown she had worn that day so, so long ago when their love had been new and Kalona had created the waterfall for her, and they had first shared their bodies with each other. At the sound of his voice, Nyx turned to face him, filling her smile with all of the love she would eternally feel for him, and wishing desperately that he would answer her smile in kind, take her into his arms, and put his anger aside.

"You should not be out here alone, especially so close to the edge of our realm," Kalona said, striding around the Wishing Tree to stand on the patch of red earth that was the Otherworld's entrance. When he finally looked at her, his amber eyes were hard.

"Has my warrior completely defeated my lover?" Nyx asked him.

He blinked in surprise. "I do not know what you mean." He approached her, obviously meaning to guide her back to the palace.

Nyx shook off his hand and walked purposefully to the hard-packed dirt at the edge of her realm. Kalona simply crossed his arms over his chest and watched her.

"Do you understand that I love you?" she asked him.

Again, surprise flickered through his amber gaze. He nodded, not speaking.

"No. Let there be no more silence between us. Answer me, son of the moon. Do you understand that I love you?"

"Yes," he said. Then he added in an emotionless voice, "You love all of your subjects."

"And you truly think there is no difference between what I feel for you and what I feel for others?"

"Which others are we speaking of? Your vampyres or your Consort?"

"I see my answers in your questions. You do not understand that I love you, and that my warrior has defeated my lover." Nyx bowed her head, steeling herself.

"I do not understand you at all anymore," Kalona said.

Nyx lifted her head and met his eyes. "Kalona, my warrior and lover, I have not changed. You have."

"No! I am as I always have been!" He almost spat the words at her. "I have never wanted to share you with Erebus."

"He is not my lover!"

"So you have said, over and over again. Yet you always, *always* turn to him over me."

"Kalona, your mind is so filled with jealousy and anger that you can no longer think clearly."

"Have you ever considered that perhaps I have only begun to think *clearly*?"

"Oh, Kalona, no. Can you not see yourself? Where has your joy gone?"

"You killed it when you chose him over me!"

"I have never done that," Nyx said. "Tell me what I can do to help rid you of the anger that is destroying you and to find your joy in our love again."

"Get rid of Erebus."

Though she had been expecting Kalona to eventually ask that very thing of her, still Nyx felt the shock to the core of her being. "Your brother was created to be my friend and playmate, as you were created to be my warrior and lover."

"I cannot bear this any longer. I will not share you!" Kalona went to Nyx and dropped to his knees, his emotion overflowing as tears washed his face. "As your warrior and lover, I beseech you. Choose me. Banish Erebus so that you and I can spend eternity together without this Darkness between us. If you do not, I vow that I will leave this realm and the despair it has caused me."

Nyx stared down at him with equal measure of sadness and resignation. "Kalona, I will not banish Erebus. Not now. Not ever."

Kalona's tears dried and his expression went to stone. "If you think I merely threaten, you are wrong."

"I believe your vow. I know you have made your choice," Nyx said. "Know that wherever you are, whatever you do, I eternally will love you, but I have made my choice as well. I will not banish Erebus. By your own vow, Kalona, you must go."

"Don't do this! You are mine!"

"I do nothing, Kalona. You have a choice in this. I have given even my warriors free will, though I don't require them to use it wisely." Tears coursed down Nyx's cheeks, soaking the gown she'd picked with such loving care.

"I cannot help myself. I was created to feel this. It is not free will. It is preordination," he said, his voice spiteful.

"Yet as your Goddess I tell you what you are is not pre-ordained. Your will has fashioned you." Though her shoulders shook with the force of her heartbreak, Nyx was filled with the unflinching power of a Goddess.

"I cannot help how I feel! I cannot help what I am!"

Nyx's words were choked, but the command in them was not diminished. "You, my warrior, are mistaken; therefore, you must pay the consequences of your mistake."

Flooded by regret and tears and despair, Nyx gathered her Divine Energy and hurled the consequences of his own choice at him, knocking him backward with such force that he was lifted from the ground and flung down, down, into the black of the ether that separated the realms.

Kalona fell.

Slowly, sadly, Nyx made her way back to her palace and all the way to her bedchamber before she collapsed onto the floor, sobbing as if her soul were broken.

The cat brought Erebus to her. He lifted Nyx in his arms as if she weighed no more than a child. He carried her to her bed, where he washed her face with a cool cloth and coaxed her into drinking some wine. Only after she had stopped weeping did he ask, "He is gone?"

Nyx nodded, eyes dark with grief. "He left me."

Erebus took her hands in his. "I will help you get him back."

"Thank you, my friend," she said tremulously. "But I will not allow him to return until he has earned forgiveness for the wrongs that he has done and the wrongs that he will do."

"Agreed," Erebus said. "Some day in the future I will help him earn your forgiveness."

"He will not let you help him."

"Then he will not know that I do."

Nyx turned her head and stared out the window of her balcony at the lush beauty that was the Otherworld and wiped at the single tear that had newly escaped her eye.

Far below, Kalona's hand perfectly mirrored the Goddess's, but his cheek was not wet with tears. Instead, catching a glimpse of himself in the still waters of the lazy creek, he saw that the moonlight color of his wings had changed to the black of the Darkness he had allowed entrance into Nyx's Otherworld.

Filled with insatiable rage, Kalona roared his anger to the night's sky and lost himself completely.

The end
For now . . .